YOURS, STERLING

YOURS, STERLING

SYDNEY WINWARD

This is a work of fiction. Names, characters, places, and incidents are either the product of the author's imagination or are used fictitiously, and any resemblance to actual persons living or dead, business establishments, events, or locales, is entirely coincidental.

Yours, Sterling

To all my awesome beta readers

Books by Sydney Winward

The Bloodborn Series
Bloodborn
Bloodbond
Bloodscourge
Bloodbane

Sunlight and Shadows Series
A Breath of Sunlight
A Taste of Shadows
A Glimpse of Music

Letters to Love Series
Yours, Sterling
Forever, Mirabelle

Lord Death Series
A Waltz with Lord Death

Novellas
Through Wylder Meadows
Root Brew Float
On Silver Wings
Bloodmoon

PROLOGUE

Sterling Winfield's heart momentarily ceased beating as he laid eyes on a beautiful woman across the ballroom. Elegant honey-brown waves draped down her back, brushing against a blue and green ball gown with a bodice that pushed everything up quite nicely, tapered at a slim waist, and dripped to the floor like shimmering water.

The woman moved gracefully across the dance floor with her partner, blue eyes shining radiantly and her smile tying his stomach in knots. Her fingers... Her wrists... Her arms... They moved with a natural-born elegance, as if she had slipped dancing from the womb.

Her partner twirled her in the middle of the room, and his breath hitched at the way she seemed to float on air as her skirt fanned out around her. She was a shining star. A sparkling moon. A whisper of beauty on a breath of wind.

"That's Kathleen de Clare," his guard Gilberd said a step behind him, startling him out of his daze, "if you care to know."

"I wasn't looking at her," he defended, but even then, his gaze refused to tear itself away from her lithe form.

After a few moments, Gilberd continued, "She's the daughter of an esteemed businessman, the eldest of five sisters. And..." The man paused for dramatic effect. "She's unattached."

An anxious breath stuttered from his lungs as he continued to watch her practically float across the room. He'd never seen anyone more beautiful in his life.

Kathleen de Clare...

"Ask her to dance." Gilberd gently nudged his arm, but Sterling bit his lip with uncertainty. "You outrank her partner. He'll be forced to give her up."

Still, he hesitated.

"How do you know who she is?"

"I know who everyone is. It's my job."

"How old is she?"

"Eighteen."

Two years older than him. He was sixteen but he might as well be thirteen.

He crossed his arms, hugging himself tight around the waist. Kathleen would never look twice at him. He had yet to have a growth spurt, so she was likely taller than him. He hadn't seen a single hair on his face or chest to indicate he was on the path to manhood. And he feared witnessing a look of disappointment or disdain on her face should he ask her for a dance.

His admiration transitioned into wistful longing. Years ago, he had despised the very mention of marriage. But now? Now he realized it was a stake a claim or lose what you want kind of game. His parents gave him the freedom to choose who he wanted as a bride, warning him that if he didn't make a decision within the next two years, they would make it for him.

"What is she like?" he asked quietly, not wanting to bring attention to himself. Though, judging by several people glancing in his direction, he reckoned he made quite the stir with a crown sitting atop his head, the only royal to make an appearance at the event. The other guests only stayed their distance because Gilberd had not given them permission to approach. Not yet.

"Uh...well..." Gilberd cleared his throat, and the hesitation drew Sterling's focus from Kathleen to his guard. "She is extroverted, loves the outdoors, she enjoys painting and riding, and from what I've heard from castle gossip, she's looking for a husband."

"Then what are all of your dramatics about? What's wrong with her?"

"Nothing is wrong with her. She just…has a reputation for a quick temper."

"Is that all?"

The guard cleared his throat again and scratched his bearded cheek. "She is also known for her long trail of broken-hearted suitors. To put it into words, she is ruthless when she wants to be."

"Ah."

Kathleen seemed to possess many great qualities for a future queen. Painting took patience. The love of outdoors and riding suggested a love of adventure. An extroverted ruler would be a great asset to securing allies and friendships. A quick temper, he thought he could live with. But the possibility of rejection should he try to stake a claim?

He glanced down at himself and frowned. Wooing the woman was not currently an option. His crown might entice her. But his physical appearance? It might send her running.

But a lot could happen in two or three years in regard to his growth. By the time he was ready to marry, perhaps he might look the part of worthy suitor rather than boyish fancy.

The song ended, and Kathleen dipped into a curtsy, several strands of her hair falling to the side to reveal the smooth, flawless skin of her neck. Her partner took her hand and kissed her fingers. More than anything, he wished to be the one taking her hand and leading her in a dance, her lovely eyes captivated by his own.

He couldn't help but watch as she returned to her group of friends, each giggling and speaking in hushed whispers to one another. When a song started up, another man asked Kathleen for a dance and whisked her across the room, this time behind several couples to shroud her from his vision.

Kathleen was a popular dance partner. He didn't doubt she was highly sought after in courtship as well.

Nearby, he overheard a group of men laughing and jesting with one another. One of them swirled the liquid in his glass and eyed Kathleen in a slightly different manner than himself, with lust in his eyes rather than admiration.

"Then why aren't you dancing with her, Lord Rupert?" One of the men laughed and punched him in the shoulder so amber liquid spilled out of his glass.

"I am practically engaged to the woman," Lord Rupert replied. "I don't need to dance with her. I know where I stand. Surely, her father will agree to the match."

Sterling balled his hands into fists when he realized just how sought after Kathleen was. If he didn't act. He would lose his chance altogether.

Curses!

He had no choice but to face her in a body that wasn't quite ready for her. At least he found a measure of satisfaction in knowing she couldn't turn away his advances in a room full of onlookers. His station as heir to a throne far outranked not only her but her dance partner as well. It would save his pride should she find him lacking.

Unless she truly was as ruthless as Gilberd seemed to think she was.

Taking a deep breath, he steeled his nerves and dug deep within himself for the courage he needed to face this beautiful, elegant, flower-breathing dragon. He took one step onto the dance floor, and then another, until he found himself weaving in and out of dancing couples.

However, when people started to notice him, the couples moved out of the way, creating a path for him as they watched his movements. Kathleen was only two couples away now...

Something slammed into him, and he crashed onto the floor, landing hard on his elbows. His crown skittered to the floor, but before he could reach it in his momentary daze, someone snatched it up and helped him to his feet.

"Forgive me, Prince Sterling," the man said as he guided him to the side of the dance floor while handing back his crown. "It's my fault. I didn't see you."

The blue of the man's eyes looked familiar, and with a start, he realized they looked similar to Kathleen's. "What is your name?"

"Theodore de Clare, Your Highness."

The hope of good fortune alighted in his chest as he placed the crown back onto his head and straightened it over his brow. "And did you bring anyone with you tonight?"

The man nodded and gestured with a hand toward the dance floor. "My eldest daughter, Kathleen, and my second eldest, Millie. Both are officially out in society."

Sterling glanced over his shoulder to find Gilberd slowly edging along the ballroom, somehow managing to move about unseen despite his large stature. He couldn't wait for his guard to catch up. He needed to take advantage of this opportunity immediately.

"May I speak to you privately?"

A seriousness lined Theodore's pinched mouth as if fearing retribution for knocking him to the ground. Still, he gave him a forced smile. "Of course. I believe there are a few rooms just down the hallway."

He followed the older man out of the ballroom, down a hallway, and into an empty room, closing the door behind them. Mr. de Clare lit a lamp, lighting a small library in a warm glow.

For what seemed like once in his life, he didn't feel anxiety over his physical insecurities. Because he knew what he wanted, and he was determined to get it. To get *her*. "I know this is sudden, but…I would like to marry your daughter, Kathleen de Clare."

Theodore froze as if taken aback by his request. The man's gaze dragged from his toes to the top of his head. "Please do not take this the wrong way, Your Highness. But have you…come of age?"

"Well…" He scratched the back of his neck. "I will be of age in two years. However, I know of engagements that have lasted far longer." He pretended to fix a crooked crown if only to draw the man's attention to it. "I am next in line to become King of Edilann. Kathleen would be a queen. What's two years in comparison to a lifetime in an influential position of power?"

A long breath escaped Theodore's lips as he leaned back against the desk and stared at him, his gaze far away as if deep in thought. After what felt like the longest time, Sterling thought he wouldn't say anything. But finally, the man spoke.

"I am a businessman, Prince Sterling. I can recognize a good, fair deal when I see it." He unfolded his arms and nodded. "I agree to a tentative betrothal. When you come of age, you and my daughter will marry. But *only* if we have not received a better offer for her hand."

What could possibly be better than the promise of a king? Or future king, for that matter? Therefore, Sterling held out his hand and the two of them shook on the deal.

"Just between you and I, if you will," Theodore said with his mouth pinched once again. "I do not want this to become public knowledge until it is made official in two years. Allow my daughter to enjoy the next two years with friendships and suitors and whatever else might make her happy."

Sterling grinded his teeth together at the thought of Kathleen courting anyone other than him. "I do not believe this is how betrothals work, Mr. de Clare. Either we are engaged, or we are not."

"I think it's more than fair. If you will have her wait two years for you, then you must allow her to grow and thrive as anyone her age ought to. I will turn away suitors who try to get too serious. Unless I see a better offer in them, of course."

Unfortunately, Sterling recognized the wisdom in the man's words. Who was he to deprive Kathleen two years' worth of happiness while waiting on a sixteen-year-old fiancé to grow up? Sterling wasn't ready to court her. Not yet. Not like this. But he knew without a doubt he wanted to marry her, so therefore, he was staking his claim.

"Then I am hoping to become one of those suitors in the coming months." They shook hands once more. "I agree to keep the betrothal a secret for now. But I expect you to remain good on your word."

"I swear I will. I am a fair and honest businessman and never go back on my word."

Sterling exited the room, only to find Gilberd standing against the wall several doors away down the hallway. If he knew what went on behind the closed door, he said nothing as Sterling passed and returned to the ballroom.

But then his heart squeezed painfully tight when Kathleen exited at the same time with her friend at her side. They bumped shoulders, close enough for him to capture the flowery scent wafting from her hair.

She giggled with an elegant hand covering her mouth and dipped into a curtsy. "Pardon me." She glanced at his crown and smiled. "Your Highness."

He stared at her smiling mouth and his heart stuttered at the beautiful sound of her laughter as she carried on her way. He begged himself to call after her, to speak to her, to ask her for a dance. But he only managed to stare dumbstruck, admiring the way she moved, the way her skirts swished around her, the way her voice captured his soul like an enrapturing melody.

"Kingdom's Glory," Gilberd muttered behind him. "You are in trouble, Sterling."

The spell broken, he turned and scowled at his guard. "Not a word, Gilberd. Not a word."

And then Kathleen disappeared around the corner, a breath of longing escaping his mouth with her sudden absence. Two years couldn't come soon enough.

Chapter One

K athleen de Clare felt as if she might retch.

She swayed on dizzy feet and leaned heavily against the railing of the *Midnight Voyager*. A gentle breeze blew tendrils of hair around her face. She closed her eyes and lifted her face to the crisp morning skies as she took a deep, calming breath.

Home...

Her heart squeezed painfully at the thought of never again seeing the beautiful gardens splayed across her father's estate. Her stomach dipped when she realized she might not witness her sisters' laughter or see them married or meet their children. And her friends...

At the thought of the many friends she'd left behind, her hand flew to her mouth. Tears pricked her eyes, but she refused to cry. Not now. Not when the crew guided the merchant ship toward land that grew larger and larger with each passing moment. She would be meeting *him* soon. For the first time. And she hardly knew a thing about him other than his name and his title.

King Sterling Winfield.

King...

Once again, her stomach churned as queasiness threw its dagger into her gut. How had she caught the eye of a king? The third prince of Armandy, Prince Nicholas, had asked her father for her hand. She had been ready to accept his suit should her father have given his blessing.

But instead of receiving it, he'd promised her hand to a stranger, dragged her onto this awful ship, and trapped her in the middle of the ocean for weeks on end.

She opened her eyes and gazed at the stream of white water trailing behind the ship. She refused to glance in the opposite direction, even for a moment. She knew what waited behind, but what waited ahead terrified her.

White fingers gripped the ship's railing too tightly, and she pried them off before they became stuck. Each joint ached from holding on for far too long.

"Kathleen," a voice startled her, and she spun to face her father. White patches weaved into the side of his brown hair. A short, weathered beard clung to his face. He watched her with a gleam of excitement, the gleam that usually appeared when he'd found a bargain at the market. The gray of his eyes stared past a loving and devoted daughter and saw the prize instead. This marriage wasn't for her. It never was.

"Stand taller. Lift your chin. Look proud. When we arrive, I want King Sterling to see a queen."

Her insides trembled. The pressure of making a fantastic first impression weighed heavily on her shoulders, especially when her stomach threatened to spill its contents over the railing. Land approached far too quickly, and the ship began slowing its pace.

"Papa." When her voice quavered, she took a deep breath and schooled her expression. "I beg you to stay for a few days. Surely, your buyer will wait a little longer."

He shook his head, his gaze shifting to the side. She made the mistake of following his gaze to the approaching port and the small specks of people gathered on Edilann's docks. Many specks. An entire cavalry of specks.

She gripped the railing again, if only to keep her knocking knees from collapsing.

"I will stay only long enough to witness the nuptials tomorrow morning. Then I must be off. I have important business to see to." He smiled, smoothed down her hair, and placed a kiss on the top of her head as if she were the jewel sitting on a king's ring rather than his oldest daughter. "You will make him a good wife and queen. You will make me proud."

At long last, the crew expertly guided the ship into Edilann's port and secured the large vessel to the docks. Anxiety grew within her, her gaze glued to the railing, which just might have indents left by her fingers. Slowly, she lifted her head. Slow…slow…slow…

Trepidation crashed into her like a lightning bolt shooting from the skies. A couple dozen soldiers stood in silver armor with Edilann's crest emblazoned on their blue cloaks—two crossed halberds surrounded by a laurel wreath. Many well-dressed courtiers spoke excitedly to one another while their gazes shot in her direction. And surrounded by a handful of guards…

Every emotion within her deflated as she gazed into a pair of wide blue eyes. The king wore a crown on top of his neat brown hair, impossible to mistake for anyone other than royalty. His baby face was more round than angular. He stood approximately a foot shorter than many of his guards.

"How old did you say he was?" she hissed at her father, her glare shooting daggers at him. Every bit of her previous anxiety was replaced by anger and disappointment and denial. "That can't possibly be King Sterling. Surely, he must be the king's younger brother." Except, she knew Sterling had no siblings. "Cousin, perhaps?"

"Hush now," her father said. He pasted on his diplomatic smile as they began their descent down the walkway, arm in arm. Her ladies maid, Mauve, followed not too far behind. "He is your same age."

She studied the king again, noting the lanky body, the awkward hunch of his shoulders, the nervousness in the set of his mouth. "Surely not." He looked like a boy. Not a man.

"He is eighteen. You are twenty. Close enough in age."

Eighteen? She peeked another glance at him and frowned. *Fifteen is more like it.*

She turned away with indifference, watching a flock of birds race across the sky instead of meeting her fiancé's gaze. "How could you approve of this match?" she asked quietly through her teeth. "What about Prince Nicholas of Armandy? I thought you would approve of the union. I'm sure you still can. We can politely decline—"

"Prince Nicholas is a third prince. He may be wealthy, but he will never be king. Sterling Winfield is already a king. It is an advantageous match."

"But Father—"

"Enough!" he hissed, dropping his diplomatic smile for a mere moment in favor of a glare directed at her. She shied away from his anger and bowed her head in submission to stare at the ground near her feet. "This is who you will marry. I will hear no more of it from you."

The king stepped forward to receive them. Her father bowed deeply, and with a slight cough, he ordered her to show the same respect. She curtsied and once again allowed her gaze to roam over him when she straightened. He wasn't only shorter than the guards, he was shorter than her, too, by a few inches.

An image surfaced in her mind of standing in front of the entire court and towering above her own husband. Heat burned her cheeks.

"I am…" King Sterling started with uncertainty in his tone. He couldn't keep his gaze on her for more than a few seconds. "I am happy to meet you, finally, Miss Kathleen." He addressed her arm rather than her face.

A not-so-kind retort rested on her tongue, and she nearly let it slip when he met her gaze.

A remnant of haunted pain lingered in his eyes, and she lowered her gaze to the ground when it reminded her of the reason why she was here, of why he was king. His parents had only recently been assassinated. According to Edilann's laws, in order to take the throne, he had to marry.

It seemed neither of them had a choice in the matter. But again, the question arose. Why had he chosen her?

"The pleasure is all mine, Your Highness," she murmured, the thorny comment dying upon her lips.

"You must be tired. After your long journey. Come home with me…and you can rest."

Home…

Her heart cried out with anguish as she slipped her arm into his and followed him to the waiting carriage. Edilann was not her home. The very air where she was from tasted of sweet berries. This air tasted crisp and dry. The people dressed in unfamiliar styles with unfamiliar hats and unfamiliar waistlines on unfamiliar bodices. An unfamiliar man—boy—walked beside her toward unfamiliar guards who escorted them to an unfamiliar carriage.

She longed to glance behind her toward the only thing that still held a flicker of home, the *Midnight Voyager*. But she stoically stared forward. Today, she would not cry.

No matter how much she longed to.

Supper passed in uncomfortable silence when dread clung to the very air. Between Mr. de Clare, Kathleen, and himself there was so much to say, but no one who wanted to say it.

Sterling's leg bounced, more than once rattling the silverware on the table. Nothing was going to plan. Absolutely nothing. He'd set this marriage in motion two years ago with every expectation to be…well…a man by now. When he'd envisioned himself waiting for her at the port, he'd seen himself as a confident, strong, tall man.

Heat climbed his neck when he caught Kathleen's gaze roaming over him for the dozenth time. Unlike at the docks, her gaze passed thoughtfully over him rather than an expression filled with disappointment.

He quickly ducked his head as a surge of bashfulness dumped its hot contents over his brow. What was wrong with him? He wasn't always so…unsure of himself. But ever since he'd become king, he feared making even the slightest mistake. That included with women. More specifically, a very beautiful, very intimidating woman. Long honey-brown hair curled to her lower back. Deep blue eyes. A soft curve to her lips.

Panic gripped his heart in the form of weaving, thorny anxiety. He met Gilberd's eye where the captain of the guard stood at the large double oak doors of the dining room, hand resting on the hilt of his sword. Gilberd motioned with his head toward Kathleen. In response, he ever so slightly shook his head.

The captain rolled his eyes and motioned again, mouthing, *Your future wife.*

Yes, that was the terrifying part.

But he knew he had to say something. As far as first glances were going, he was struggling with making a favorable impression.

Say something, you dunderhead.

He lifted his head again as he pooled in every sliver of bravery he possessed, only to find the other two staring at him expectantly. His heart stopped. Ice burned his lungs.

"Would you like me to repeat my question?" Kathleen asked with an unrepentant smirk gracing her mouth. "Or would you like to continue staring at the table?"

"Kathleen," Mr. de Clare hissed.

Sterling's face paled. "I-I-I'm sorry. What did you say?"

"I asked if you ride. I enjoy riding myself."

He sighed in relief. Familiar territory. "I do enjoy it. There is…a nice trail I like to take through the forest."

She leaned forward and pierced him with stunning blue eyes. His heart took a dive off the castle wall and landed with a splat all over the cobblestone walkway. "Riding is a great way for two people to get to know each other better."

Thinking of how often he'd gone riding with Gilberd, he nodded his head. "Yes, it is."

"More specifically, two newly acquainted people. A husband and wife, for example."

He paused for a moment, the entire room a chilling, expectant hush. Did he miss something? Did he not just answer her question? "Yes…it is?"

"Oh my," she huffed as she stood and threw her napkin onto the table, her food hardly touched. "If you will excuse me, I've found myself in need to have a conversation with the garden trellis. It will be much more eventful than this."

With another huff, she spun on her heel and stormed past Gilberd and out of the room, flanked by a couple of Edilann guards. His jaw dropped as he watched her disappear in a raging sea of green and white skirts. What had he said wrong?

"Forgive her, Your Highness," Mr. de Clare said as he stood and bowed several times. "She's weary from her travels. She will be bright and amiable tomorrow for the wedding after a good night's rest."

The man kept his head bowed in submission like a dog hoping not to get kicked after tearing apart a piece of furniture.

With a deflated heart, Sterling folded his napkin and placed it on top of the table. He hadn't touched his food either. "Excuse me."

As he moved toward the door, an entourage of guards started to move with him, but with a silent command from Gilberd, they retreated and instead, he accompanied him into the hallway. Torches tossed light across dark walls, shadows flickering across sconces, paintings, and draperies. The hallways were empty aside from the occasional bowing noble perusing the castle.

Upon a particularly empty stretch of hallway, Gilberd said, "How could you miss her hint?"

"What hint?" He threw an annoyed glance in the other man's direction. Gilberd was fifteen years his senior with a full beard spread across his face and careful eyes that constantly scanned the path ahead.

"Miss Kathleen wanted you to ask her to go riding with you."

"Oh." He ran a hand over his face and released a sigh. "I have exactly zero experience with women. How was I supposed to know what she wanted?"

Gilberd tapped Sterling's head like a friend would rather than a loyal and dedicated guardsman. They'd become close during the rough transition from prince to king. "Women think differently than men. You have to catch their hidden meanings. And quickly. You've got a woman with a temper on your hands. Good luck, Your Highness."

"Lower your voice," he whispered, glancing back and forth across empty hallways. "I have enough on my plate without having to deal with her overhearing you say that as well."

Gilberd smirked. "What did you expect? Bringing a spitfire like her to the castle? She has a reputation, you know."

"I know."

A reputation for many spurned and broken-hearted suitors. A reputation for speaking her mind rather than keeping her mouth shut. A reputation for a quick temper.

"But you should have seen her." He sighed as he approached a window overlooking the gardens. He leaned against the window frame and gazed out over the vast amount of greens, pinks, reds, and yellows bathed underneath pale, glowing moonlight. "She was and still is beautiful. She was the most elegant dancer. I couldn't tear my gaze away. I don't care that she's older than me. When I saw her, I wanted her to be mine." A flush crept up his neck as he kept his eyes glued to a patch of white flowers slowly opening their petals to the moon's embrace. "It sounds silly when I say it out loud."

"Not at all silly." The captain joined him at the window, never once taking his hand off his sword. "When I saw my wife for the first time, I was struck dumb. Mirabelle was courting someone else at the time. Waiting for my turn was painful."

"And you've been together for a while now."

"Yes, we—"

"Shh!" Sterling hissed moments before he ducked out of view of the window. His heart pounding, he peeked around the corner just as Kathleen came into view with her guards trailing behind. His knees weakened as he watched her bend over a bush filled with pink roses to inhale their sweet scent. A soft smile eased her tense expression into serenity.

A lump formed in his throat as she trailed an elegant hand over the petals. How could he ever be good enough to stand by her side? Especially looking like *this*? Of course, he didn't consider himself ugly by any means. But he looked younger than he truly was, and Kathleen... Well, she was beautiful and graceful and perfect. He didn't care about her reputation. He knew she had a sweet, gentle heart. He'd witnessed it two years earlier just as he witnessed it right now.

"I don't want her outside when it's this dark," Gilberd murmured. "Not after what happened to your parents. What if Armandy assassins..."

Chilling ice traveled through each one of his veins. Worry for his betrothed spurred his legs into action as he walked swiftly toward the nearest door leading to the gardens. "You don't think... They couldn't possibly get through our security again."

"They did it once." Gilberd followed only a step behind him. "They met their goal, so returning to Edilann seems unlikely. But I wouldn't be too careless."

Before Sterling exited the door, Gilberd held out a cautioning arm. "Allow me, Your Highness. Keeping you safe is my top priority."

The captain motioned for another guard, Raimbaut, to take his place at Sterling's side before he met the other three outside. A nervous trickle of sweat dripped down Sterling's forehead for an entirely different reason than his upcoming wedding. Kathleen was his responsibility now. He needed to keep her safe. If she ever got hurt… He would never forgive himself.

Only after she was escorted safely inside and to her bedchambers did he relax. He couldn't lose another person he cared for. It would utterly break him.

Chapter Two

This was it. Today was the first day of the rest of her life.

Kathleen studied her reflection in the full-length mirror, turning back and forth to admire the way her silk blue dress shimmered in the light entering from the window. The lace trim on the bottom of the dress and sleeves matched her lacy veil, a veil in which she wanted to hide behind for the duration of the ceremony.

She twisted a strand of her honey-brown hair around her finger, but Mauve smacked the strand out of her hand as if telling her to stop playing with it. She had known the woman all her life, and they were closer than a princess and a servant ought to be.

"Stop fidgeting," Mauve ordered, and she glared.

"Fidgeting is better than pondering my future."

"Your future is sealed, Miss Kathleen. You must choose to be happy with the sudden turn of events."

Scoffing, she turned her attention away from the mirror. "I am marrying a child."

"The young king is not a child. He is eighteen years old."

"And I am twenty."

"Age will mean very little in a few years."

She couldn't help but roll her eyes and turned her glare toward the long blue sleeves covering her arms. "What happens in a few years? Most men his age are fully grown. He barely makes it past my shoulder."

Alright, so it wasn't completely true. He was a few inches shorter than her, but because she planned to wear the tallest heels she could find just to spite her father and this marriage, Sterling would barely make it past her shoulder.

The silver heels looked nice on her feet, accentuating every graceful dip and curve. The feet of a dancer, her mother had always told her. Although she'd known the day she'd marry would come sooner or later, she hadn't been ready to say goodbye to her mother's grave and her younger sisters so quickly.

Her ladies maid clicked her tongue as she fussed with the veil so it hung just right in the back. "Must you humiliate your fiancé? There is no logical reason for you to stand so much taller than him."

"There is every reason. I am marrying a *child*. I could have married a wealthy duke or an attractive foreigner. But instead I am stuck playing nursemaid." She didn't mention Nicholas again. The disappointment was too great, and she was far too upset and angry at having the expectations of her future ripped out from under her, her choice taken away entirely. But who was she most upset at?

Her father for using her for his own political gain?

Nicholas for not fighting harder to keep her?

Or Sterling for not making any effort to woo her before this marriage?

"Sterling is a *king*. There is no better match for you. You know it. Your family knows it. King Sterling knows it."

"But why me?" After Sterling's parents were killed by assassins, he had inherited the throne, and shortly after, her father had informed her that a deal had been struck. She would wed the new king.

"*You should count yourself lucky,*" her younger sister had scolded. "*Not every man can suck up his pride enough to marry a woman two years his senior.*"

Mauve smiled. "Why wouldn't he choose you?" She placed her hands on Kathleen's shoulders and turned her to face the mirror again. "You are beautiful. You are graceful. You are talented. Everything a man wants in a bride. Had His Highness asked for your hand even two weeks later, you would have been spoken for. He was wise to make a claim for you when he did."

"I might have married the third prince of Armandy if Sterling had kept his claim to himself." Fine, so she couldn't help herself from mentioning Nicholas.

Her heart panged at the thought, an echo in the suddenly vast cavern in her chest. She'd had every reason to believe her father would accept Nicholas's suit. She recalled the sunshine on her face as she and the third prince had strolled in the garden together back home. Beneath the gazebo overlooking the lake, he'd kissed her. And her heart had responded with warmth and song. Perhaps, she was not so disappointed with Sterling's age or youthful appearance. But in the loss of what could have been with Nicholas. Now she would never know.

"Yes, but a third prince is hardly a prize for someone like you. Sterling can offer you so much more."

Prize...

She gritted her teeth at the word. She was not a person, but an object to be measured and traded. A part of her wondered how much her father had overexaggerated her good qualities to have had *two* princes vying for her hand. Her family was not titled, despite their wealth. She was exceptional at painting, and she enjoyed dancing and taking walks in the garden. But she was nothing special, and she certainly was not queen material.

She ignored the comment and admired her tall heels again for added measure. They were perfect for utter humiliation. If she had to feel the embarrassment of standing taller than her betrothed, she wanted him to feel it, too.

A knock sounded on the door, and a blanket of dread fell over her as she watched Mauve open it. From this angle, she couldn't see who stood on the other side of the threshold, but his boyish voice gave him away immediately.

"I would like to speak to Kathleen," King Sterling said.

Kathleen's eyes widened and she shook her head as she mouthed *no* over and over again, but Mauve ignored her. Instead, her ladies maid curtsied and excused herself from the room.

Internally groaning, she debated whether to pretend she wasn't in the room, but to avoid her soon-to-be husband on their wedding day was bad manners.

Taking a deep breath, she schooled her expression to keep her annoyance hidden. She picked up her skirts and rounded the door to find Sterling standing in the hallway.

He was cute, she supposed. Neat brown hair. Pretty blue eyes. A straight nose and an attractive mouth. But he was short. And his face was more round than angular like a man's should be. He was just a boy, and if he hadn't grown by now, he likely never would.

His eyes widened, and his cheeks reddened more by the second as his gaze darted to her heels and traveled upward to stare at the top of her head. The blush in his cheeks spread to his ears, and she had to hide her smirk of satisfaction. If he was this humiliated when they were by themselves, how humiliated would he be in front of an audience?

A small voice in the back of her mind expressed regret, but she batted it away. It was Sterling's fault she was not going to marry Nicholas, and the choice being stripped of her made her angry and upset.

"Oh, I..." He cleared his throat and looked into her eyes, but he quickly dropped his gaze to his feet. "I wanted to see you to...uh...to offer you a gift before the wedding. It's...it's not much, but I hoped you might like it."

The young king produced a pink rose from behind his back, and she inhaled a sharp breath of surprise. With gentle fingers, she took the flower from him and brought it to her nose to inhale its sweet fragrance. She brushed the silky petals and traced the long stem.

"Roses are my favorite," she murmured.

She studied him in a different light. Had she been too hard on him? While she'd been too busy being upset about her situation, she'd overlooked the obvious kindness he displayed. A goodness. An acute sense of observation. An initiative to try to make this work, even with her own reluctance dividing them. Sterling had not taken the throne by choice. What must the burden be like?

"I noticed you admiring them in the garden earlier." He cleared his throat again and rubbed the back of his flushed neck. "I, uh, suppose I should get going. The…the priest is waiting for me."

He ducked away far too quickly for her to utter a "thank you". After shutting the door behind her, she smiled as she gazed at the lovely flower in her hand. The young king was sweet—far sweeter than she had expected him to be.

Pretty eyes.

Sweet demeanor.

"I suppose I can be content enough with that," she said to herself and sighed as she lifted her skirts to reveal her heels. Never again would she be able to wear platform shoes. The thought created a vain ache within her chest. It seemed flats were the only option.

With her pink rose nestled safely inside a vase filled with water, she exchanged her heels for flats, took a deep breath, and met Sterling at the cathedral.

Kathleen gazed out over the dance floor with a mix of awe and longing. She sat at a long table at the front of the room next to her new husband and watched colorful skirts twirl around smiling gentlemen. A string quartet played in the corner, beautiful music lifting into the Great Hall and reverberating against the high-domed ceiling. Ladies and Lords bowed to one another as the dance finished and another one started. Conversations and laughter rose on either side of her, though not one peep escaped Sterling. He watched the dancers with concentration written between his brows while one leg nervously bounced up and down.

Cute, she thought again, stealing a side-glance at him.

He was not handsome, but cute. He was not burly, but scrawny. His voice was that of a boy's and not of a man's. He dressed in fine clothes, blue and gold—Edilann's colors—and his crown sat atop his head. When he sat in a chair, he didn't appear much shorter than her. But he was kind and thoughtful despite his constant fluster and his mind's tendency to disappear for many minutes at a time.

I am a married woman, she thought to herself, the shock still sinking in. The ruby and gold ring sitting on her finger attested to her new relationship status. A queen. She had never seen herself rising up the ranks to become queen. A countess, maybe. But a queen?

She smiled wryly as she looked Sterling's way again. A queen to a king who had hardly spoken two sentences to her all day, and it was their *wedding day.*

Suddenly, his knee stopped bouncing and he turned his head in her direction. Not for the first time, a blush rose to his ears. "Why are you looking at me like that?"

Not wanting to divulge her musing, she answered with another topic that had occupied her thoughts for a time. "I'm trying to imagine what it must be like for you. Only two months ago, you became king. Edilann law dictates that you must be wed upon the throne. Your life has changed so much so quickly." She paused as she contemplated asking her next question and decided to go forward with it. "Do you miss your parents?"

Melancholy drapes closed over his expression. "Yes. Very much."

"I miss my family, too." She placed her hand on the table between them just to see if he might reach out for her. He didn't. Coward? Or Oblivious? "My mother passed away several years ago, my father left the country this afternoon, and my sisters are back home. They aren't gone from this world like your family, but I will not be able to see them often anymore."

If it was possible to become smaller, he managed it with hunched shoulders and clasped hands. "It…it must be difficult. Being…being a woman. To depart from your…from your family."

The tone of his voice sounded apologetic and uncertain, and his gaze didn't leave his lap. A flare of annoyance caught onto the kindling inside her, and she picked up her napkin to fan her face as she tried to hide her emotions. The person before her was not a king. He was a boy who didn't know how to assert himself.

She decided to give him a couple of chances to try.

"The dancers are beautiful," she commented, looking out over the dance floor and watching as the couples circled one another with only wrists touching. "I adore dancing."

His knee started bouncing again, his fingers now fiddling with his dessert fork. He nodded absently, but otherwise said nothing in reply. His guard, the one with the beard, coughed into his hand from where he stood several feet behind them.

Breathing in slowly and letting it out even slower, she doused her temper with a swig of wine from her goblet. She tried again. "If only a fine gentleman would ask me to dance. I think I could probably dance all night."

Instead of asking her as she hoped, the skin between his brows crinkled, and his knee continued to bounce. Her temper burst into flames within her, and she slammed her goblet down, rattling the silverware on the table. Sterling jumped in his seat, his eyes wide as he stared back at her.

"Can my hints be any subtler?" she asked, and she knew she either needed to get out of her seat or find a patch of fresh air, otherwise she might implode further. "I am wanting you to ask me to dance."

His face reddened, promptly followed by a flush down his neck. "You want to dance with me?"

"You are my husband, are you not?"

"Yes, but—"

"Sterling Winfield, if you do not ask me to dance in the next ten seconds—"

"Dance with me?" He held out a hand to her, and although the uncertainty remained in his eyes, she also noticed something she had not yet seen. Hope.

She quickly doused her remaining temper and frustration. He was trying. So could she. She just had to remind herself that they weren't well-acquainted with one another yet. It might take more time for him to converse and act comfortably with her.

She slid her fingers into his and smiled as he gently pulled her to her feet. His hand warmed hers as he guided her across the floor, all eyes on them. Many couples stopped dancing, and others standing on the edge of the dance floor watched expectantly. Sterling ducked his head as if he disliked the attention, while she thrived on it.

Although the previous set was not yet over, the musicians stopped mid-note and began a new song.

Sterling took her by the waist, the space between his brows crinkling with concentration—another endearing quality she added to the short list of things she liked about him. She hoped, with time, the list would grow longer.

He led her in a dance, rather clumsily as if he hadn't had much practice. Fortunately, she was an experienced dancer herself and used her twirling dress to mask his choppy movements.

When he glanced up, he stumbled and would have smashed her foot if she hadn't moved quickly enough to avoid it. "Everyone is staring at us," he murmured.

Indeed, all other dancers had stopped and stood watching at the edge of the ballroom, leaving her and her new husband as the only two dancing. Her heart fanned alive at the undivided attention, and she became more confident in her steps.

They turned in a circle, and her surroundings melded into a green, blue, and yellow blur as music filled her ears like a ribbon of golden notes. A smile spread across her face. "It's our wedding day, Sterling. Of course, they're watching us."

The crease between his brows returned, and when his attention lingered on their audience, she released his hand for a moment to touch his face, gently pulling his attention back to her. Soft and smooth as a baby's bottom. He probably couldn't grow facial hair even if he tried.

His mouth lifted in a half-smile—the first she'd seen since they'd met. Her heart gave a surprising skip, and she couldn't help but return his smile with one of her own. She added "cute smile" to her list.

When she raised her hand with the intention of placing it into his again, he grunted and jerked away from her suddenly. Her heart dropped to her toes. Horror filled her expression when she noticed the arrow protruding from his right shoulder. Red quickly spread across his chest. He fell to his knees, gasping in pain only moments before the room erupted into chaos. People screamed, jostling each other in an attempt to run to safety.

Terror iced over her heart and tempted her to flee for her own safety, but the rational part of her brain broke through just enough for her to rush to Sterling's side. She draped his left arm over her shoulders and wrapped an arm around his waist, hefting him to his feet. Frightened screams echoed in her ears as her gaze darted for an exit, but too many people blocked her path.

"Just hold on, Sterling," she said, words strained, but she couldn't even hear her own voice over the mayhem.

He grunted again, and his legs collapsed on him when they took several steps forward. She might have dropped him if a couple of guards hadn't appeared right then. One carefully took his right side, the other his left, and they shielded her with their bodies while rushing toward the servants' passageway.

The sound of clashing swords followed them before the guards sealed the passageway behind them. Darkness engulfed them, only a lone torch lighting their way. One guard grabbed it from the wall, and the flickering shadows danced across their feet while they traversed the long and narrow halls and stairways. Finally, they reached what looked to be the kitchen, and the guards eased Sterling into a chair.

She bit her knuckle to keep from crying. His blood soaked nearly his entire shirt, and by default from having helped him earlier, it soaked one side of her bodice as well.

"Fetch water and fresh cloths!" a guard ordered a couple of frightened kitchen servants before turning back to Sterling. "Your Highness, I am going to pull the arrow out. Bite down on this." He placed a leather hide between his teeth.

In a motion quicker than a strike of lightning, the guard yanked the arrow out, and Sterling released a muffled cry. This time, her tears did escape. She clamped her hand over her mouth in an attempt to stifle a strangled sob.

He cried out again when the guard poured alcohol over the wound. Her hand reached for his, and she gave it a firm squeeze. It felt cold and clammy.

As the guard began tying a bandage around the wound, the guard with the beard burst inside, flecks of blood spattered on his uniform. "Your Highness," he gasped, breathing heavily. "Soldiers from Armandy have managed to sneak across our border. Some are here inside the castle. I dispatched a unit to deal with the ones who haven't yet crossed the bridge."

An arrow of shock shot into her own shoulder. Armandy? But Nicholas was the country's prince. He and his family couldn't be responsible for this. They just couldn't.

Sterling's face paled even more. "Armandy assassins killed my parents." His attention snapped to her, a surprising amount of clarity in his eyes. Clarity and fear. "You must flee the city. I'll send a dozen soldiers as protection."

"Sterling, no." Another strangled sob escaped her, and she squeezed his hand tighter. "I won't leave you." Not like this. Not on their wedding day. Not when she didn't know whether he would live or die tonight.

"You must. I could never forgive myself if they killed you, too."

The bearded guard with blood on his uniform said, "The path to the back road is clear. We'll take her that way."

He nodded and lowered his voice. "Gilberd, escort her to Summit Abbey. Tell no one of her whereabouts."

"Sterling, *no*." Tears trailed down her face, and she didn't bother wiping them away. "I don't want to go. I want to stay with you." She surprised herself by speaking the truth. She wanted to stay with her new husband.

With a weak squeeze to her hand, he gave her a sorrowful look, followed by a grimace of pain. "I will send word as soon as I can. I pray you will have a safe journey."

Gilberd placed a hand on her elbow and steered her away. "We must go now, Your Highness, while you still have a window to flee."

She looked back one last time to see the devastation in Sterling's eyes as he returned her gaze. The memory stayed with her when she threw a dark blue cloak over her head and allowed the guards to escort her into the darkness of night. The quiet efficiency in which they harnessed a horse to a carriage astounded her, but not for long as a numbness climbed up her body and seized her heart. Gilberd helped her inside the carriage, and it jolted forward.

Even in the darkness, the blood covering her hand was visible, and a new fear crept over the numbness—a fear for Sterling.

A single tear dripped down her chin. She parted the curtains the slightest bit to peer out the window, but the castle had already fallen behind, out of sight.

"Don't you *dare* leave me a widow on our wedding day," she whispered into the darkness, but only silence answered back.

Chapter Three

K athleen awoke as the carriage came to an abrupt halt, knocking her head against the glass window. She squinted against the bright light entering through the curtains and breathed in cold air.

Cold?

A chill entered her bones, and she rubbed her hands up and down her arms in an attempt to warm herself and still her shivering limbs. When she exhaled, a foggy breath escaped her lips. She pulled her cloak tighter around herself.

Someone knocked on the carriage door moments before it opened, and a chilly draft entered as a flurry of snow burst inside. The white specks clung to her hair and eyelashes, and her shivering worsened. Snow… It was nearly summer! Where were they that snow could reach them?

A guard she recognized as Gilberd poked his head inside, his reddish-brown beard covered in white flakes. The tip of his nose flared red as if a bitter wind had nipped at him for several hours straight.

"Your Highness," he said, his words stinted by numb lips. "The carriage can no longer make it up the snowy pass. The abbey is not far now. But you will need to ride a horse."

"Take me back," she demanded in as authoritative a tone as she could muster after just waking up, though her voice still croaked with grogginess.

"I apologize, my queen," he replied with a dip of his head, "but I am under King Sterling's orders. You will not be able to return until he commands it."

The man's words angered her. All her life, everyone else had made all her decisions. What to wear. Who to befriend. What parties to attend. Who to marry. Just this once, she wanted to decide for herself. And she wanted to return to Sterling.

"And should my husband die?"

"Then we will personally escort you back down the mountain."

She opened her mouth to argue, but instantly regretted it when she choked on a gust of icy wind. It was as if he took it as an agreement because he grasped her by the elbows and hoisted her out of the carriage and onto the back of a chestnut mare. The moment she gained her balance, he draped a thick fur over her shoulders and led the horse forward by the reins.

Wind picked up the snow around them and threw it in all directions like salty sea water spraying across jagged rocks. She squinted against the haze of white to find six of the twelve guards escorting her the rest of the way while the other six remained with the carriage.

Far too soon, the tips of her ears and nose ached, and frigid cold seeped into her dainty slippers. At least she hadn't worn the heels. This scenario could have been worse.

But not by much.

The horses rounded the bend, and finally, a tall structure came into view. The gray stones rose high in the air and stretched across the plateaued mountain. No flags adorned the top of the structure, but a triangle with three overlapping circles stood humbly outside the large double doors—the symbol for their deity, Mother Divine.

Summit Abbey.

The doors opened to reveal two women wearing long black and white habits and veils. A Mother Divine necklace dangled on a long chain from one of their necks.

"We seek refuge for our queen!" Gilberd shouted, his voice almost drowned in the thick wind.

They took one glance at Kathleen on the horse and nodded, ushering them inside. The guard scooped her into his arms so she didn't have to place her rudely covered feet in the snow. Warm air greeted her within the walls of the abbey, though the quick transition from freezing to warm made her fingers and toes ache with burning heat.

"Oh, the poor dear," the woman with the necklace said while leading them deeper into the abbey. "Place her in front of the fire to warm herself. And of course, you and your men are welcome to stay as long as you need to."

"Thank you, sister," he replied gruffly, and a moment later, Kathleen found herself sitting in a chair before a roaring fire. "We will rest for the night, and then we will be gone by morning."

The two women shooed the men away and fussed over her the moment they left the room. They took her shoes off and rubbed their hands over her frozen feet. Another nun entered carrying a tray with a bowl of hot broth and a steaming cup of tea.

"You may call me Sister Margaret, and this is Sister Enid," the woman with the necklace said as she placed the cup of tea in her hands. Kathleen sighed at the warmth seeping through her fingers. "What may we call you?"

Before answering, she took a sip of the tea to thaw her frigid throat. Her answer escaped as a croak. "Queen Kathleen Winfield of Edilann."

"A mouthful, to be sure," Sister Enid chuckled, the action making her wrinkles stand out on her cheeks. "We will call you Sister Kathleen. Are you in trouble, dear?" She glanced at the blood covering her dress. "Are you hurt?"

"No."

"Running away from your husband?"

Her eyes widened, and she promptly shook her head. "Heavens, no. He sent me here for my safety. The palace got attacked." The memory of his blood spreading across his shirt caused shivers to run down her spine. What was his fate? Had he survived? Would he come fetch her the moment their enemies fled? She couldn't imagine staying in the Abbey for more than a few weeks.

Sister Enid patted her cheek and smiled. "Stay as long as you need to. This is a sanctuary, but it is also a place of worship. You will need to change your clothing. And…" The sister grimaced apologetically as her gaze traveled to the crown sitting on top of her head. "Only modest jewelry is allowed."

Hiding her own grimace was no easy feat as she looked over the sisters' clothing. Black and white. Habits and veils. She could do without her crown just fine, but… "Surely, I will be able to keep my hair uncovered."

"No, dear. At the abbey, we are all equal, even you."

She touched a strand of her soft honey-brown hair, already mourning the tresses never seeing the light of day until she was to return to the palace.

It's only for a few weeks, she reminded herself. *And then my hair can bask in the sunlight again.*

She hid her ruby wedding ring from view by tucking her hand beneath her arm. She refused to take it off, no matter what they might insist. This was Sterling's ring. And just the sight of the small piece of jewelry gave her hope for his survival.

He will make it, she reassured herself as her gaze traveled to the window and the flurry of snow just outside. *He will survive.*

Three months passed. *Three.* With no word from Sterling.

Kathleen found herself pacing the halls of the abbey often, her eyes sore from either being blinded by the bright white snow outside or from having to squint in the too-dark corridors. She had already bitten her nails to nervous stubs, mourning the loss of them along with her hair she was not allowed to leave uncovered.

Every day melded into the same routine from the time she woke up, to morning prayers, to eating supper in hushed whispers. The only solace she found while staying in this dreary abbey were the two hours allotted to personal study, which she found herself a quiet corner to sketch. Paint supplies were scarce, and she dared not upset the sisters by depleting their stores.

She sat beside the warm fire and used up another precious paper in her notebook to sketch her last memory of Sterling. In the sketch, he sat in a chair in the palace kitchens, a bandage around his shoulder. His eyes held a world of fear in their depths, not for himself, but for her. But had the fear truly been for her safety? Had he cared about her enough to remove her from harm's way, or had a fear of loss caused him to send her away?

The front doors of the abbey creaked open, and the fire in front of her swayed as a cold draft entered the room. A voice rose in the hallway. A man's voice.

Slamming her notebook shut, she ignored the sisters' earlier warnings not to run in a place of worship and raced toward the front of the abbey. Several sisters greeted a man whose face was hidden by a snow-covered scarf. He slid it off from around his neck to reveal a familiar face. He was the bearded man who had accompanied her to the abbey months ago. Captain Gilberd.

Not giving him a chance to settle in near a warm fire, she approached with pleading eyes. "Sterling?"

Captain Gilberd brushed the snow off his gloves and tucked them into his coat pocket. "He's alive and well."

He motioned to a box near the door. "He sent you a letter and gifts, and regrets to inform you that you must stay here for a while longer. It's not safe to return to the palace."

Panic rose to her throat, gripping, clawing, suffocating despite her relief over Sterling's good health. She reached out to the wall to steady herself. "But winter is approaching! If I don't leave *now*, I will be stuck here for at least another five months. The passes will not be traversable."

He smiled apologetically. "His Highness sends his regrets."

"Regrets?" Her voice rose an octave. "Let's see how much regret he could muster if *he* was the one trapped on the top of a blasted mountain!"

Sister Margaret gasped. "Language, Sister Kathleen! This is a place of worship."

The captain cleared his throat and addressed the sisters. "I will speak to my queen privately, if you will."

He scooped up the box from Sterling, and Kathleen followed him into the room where she'd sketched her husband. Truly, she was relieved he was alive and well, but if she had to spend another five months in this dreadful place...

When he set the box on top of a table, she opened the lid while he warmed his hands by the fire. Inside the box lay a beautiful purple gown, a sapphire necklace, and a letter lying on top, sealed with the royal Edilann emblem—two crossed halberds surrounded by a laurel wreath. She tore the letter open first, needing the reassurance of Sterling's words.

Dear Kathleen,

I promised to send word as soon as I was able. We are now at war with Armandy, and because of that, you must remain at the abbey. The roads are not safe for a queen. The summit is the safest place for you right now.

I hope you might correspond with me in the meantime. It would pass the time quicker.

Yours, Sterling

Even in letters, he sounded uncertain, and she imagined the space between his eyebrows crinkling while he'd written it.

Armandy… So, they truly had been responsible for the attack.

Her gut clenched with discomfort as she remembered Nicholas's carefree laugh, his smile, his kiss… Had he known about or even supported the assassination of Sterling's parents? Had his family sanctioned the assassination attempt on Sterling's life?

And then her thoughts turned to Sterling. Sweet. Thoughtful. Young Sterling. Just barely come of age. He hadn't deserved that arrow.

To think she had almost married Nicholas. Would she have been happy married to a man capable of attacking another kingdom? Capable of hurting a young man of barely eighteen? What were their reasons for it? Or were the attacks simply unprovoked?

She sighed despondently as she caressed the soft fabric of the dress and traced the contours of the largest sapphire in the necklace. They were lovely gifts for royalty, but useless for a woman living at an abbey.

She lifted her head to find Captain Gilberd still lingering beside the fire, patiently waiting for her to finish reading the letter. It hadn't taken long. It was short just like every one of hers and Sterling's conversations thus far.

"We are at war?" she finally asked after she pushed her melancholy emotions to the back of her heart. "Why now? Why not after Sterling's parents were killed?"

"There was no one to declare war after their deaths," he answered, now shrugging off his coat. "And Sterling is…well, he's inexperienced. He has only known peace all his life."

An angered frown broke through her composure. Another five months at the abbey? At least? War or not, she should be beside her husband and not hiding in a fortress in the mountains.

Gilberd turned to her and gave her a pleading smile. "Go easy on him, Your Highness. He's only trying to do his best."

Her voice quieted as she held the letter against her heart, tears pooling in her eyes. "Would you have done the same to your wife?"

"This isn't about me—"

"Answer me, please."

He sighed and ran a hand over his beard. "I fear for my wife and children's safety every day. So, I fight for it. I fight for them. That is all I will say."

"Fair enough." Her chin trembled at the weight of the uncertainty. Of the loneliness. Of her world getting torn apart before it truly even began. But she tried to remain strong. "When will you return to Sterling?"

"The longer I am away, the more anxious I become. I will depart as soon as you will allow."

A part of her wanted to weep, because she knew the moment she dismissed him, she would sign away her freedom for many more months. But with a war raging on, it seemed she had no choice. So, she sat down at the desk beside the cold, drafty window, dipped a quill in ink, and touched it to paper to reply to her husband's letter.

Dear Sterling,

It saddens me to learn of the war. I pray for your safety every day. Captain Gilberd assures me that you are well and on the mend. I am glad to hear of it. The gifts you sent are lovely. Thank you.

I am happy to correspond with you. What is your favorite season? Mine is spring. It's when all the flowers bloom, the birds sing, and the sun shines after a long winter spell. What do you like to do in your spare time? I enjoy spending time outdoors myself, whether it be losing myself on a walk, painting in the garden, or taking tea on the terrace. Do you like music? I love attending an orchestra concert or listening to an opera performance from the top level of a theater.

Until I hear from you again,
Kathleen

Outdoors…

Her gaze traveled to the window and the frost building on the glass. Through the frost, she just barely made out green pines covered in layers of snow. Not a single village was within view of the window, and there were certainly no flowers poking out of the mountains of white powder.

After blotting the letter and sealing it inside an envelope, she handed it to the captain, her heart heavier than she allowed her expression to show.

"You may leave whenever you wish, Captain. Just make sure Sterling gets this."

He nodded and bowed briefly. "You have my word." He slipped his arms back into his coat, tucked the letter into an inside pocket, and he was already walking toward the door when he wrapped his scarf around his neck and face. She watched him leave with an ache in her heart as she realized she would miss autumn's leaves changing from green to red to yellow, if she hadn't already.

Five more months. She could survive this.

Chapter Four

Just when Kathleen thought the mountain couldn't possibly receive any more snow, the heavens dumped piles upon piles over the summit. The frost bit her nose as she and Sister Enid huddled in the warmth of their coats, gloves, and hats while they shoveled scoop after scoop of snow out of the way of the front door of the abbey. Despite the forlorn weather, several wounded soldiers found their way here in their escape from the enemy. Some bleeding out. Others with purple or even black appendages from the frosty temperatures.

Her mouth puckered in a frown when she spotted white snow stained red, and then her stomach dropped to her toes. The tip of a boot stuck out of the snow.

A gasp escaped her. Panic. Trepidation. Worry. She trudged through the snow until she reached the spot of red, her gloves now soaked as she dug through the powder.

Until she unearthed a face nearly as pale as the snow that buried him. A soldier from Edilann.

"Sister Enid!" she shouted, scooping handfuls of snow off the man until she uncovered the rest of his body. "Sister!"

"Oh dear," the woman murmured. Three other sisters hurried outside, and between the four of them, they lifted the man off the ground and carried him inside. When they placed him beside the fire, Kathleen knelt to check his pulse.

His heart still beat. Weakly. But he was alive.

Blood froze to his shirt, slowly dethawing beside the fire. The gray in his hair indicated he was at least forty years old. And as she and the sisters cleaned and warmed him up, Kathleen noticed his hand clenched tight in a fist. She gently pried his fingers open to reveal a silver locket. It looked as if it belonged to a woman.

The man had a sweetheart.

A sob got stuck in her throat. She dropped the man's hand and watched as several other sisters transported him to the room filled with beds. Some occupied. Others not. That man had a family, and she swore she would try to help save his life so he might return to them once more.

She sniffed back tears and turned to another man who groaned from where he lay on the corner cot. He looked to be around the age of fifteen, and he was missing his right hand, likely his sword arm.

Her heart trembled within her ribcage. The young man reminded her of Sterling. Although not quite the same age, they looked similar with a soft face, brown hair, and long eyelashes. Those same eyelashes fluttered in sleep as she changed the bandage on his stump. Her stomach turned at the horrendous sight, but she pressed on until a clean, white bandage replaced the bloodied one.

A silent prayer left her mouth, her lips moving without a sound. She prayed for Sterling and his safety. For his good health and that the war would end soon.

"Your Highness."

Hope jumped into her chest at the sound of the voice. She spun around to find Gilberd in the doorway. He wore thick furs to protect him from the outside chill, his cheeks stung pink from the bitter wind.

"You're here!" she gasped, rushing toward him. How much time had passed? Two months? She hadn't expected to see him for another three months.

At the sight of her, Gilberd released an audible sigh before motioning her toward the hearth on the opposite side of the infirmary room. He spoke quietly.

"A spy learned of your whereabouts. I dispatched him before he reached his king. I wasn't sure if anyone else found out. Sterling ordered me to check on you, frantic as he was." He chuckled and shook his head wryly. "Even in this weather. Barely made it up here."

She pressed her hands to her heart. "How is he?"

The man shrugged. "The war is taking a toll on us all. Especially during these chilly months. He's uninjured. Just…"

"Just what?" she whispered.

"Tired. We don't know when this will end."

She rested a shoulder against the wall and frowned. Five months had already passed since the attempt on Sterling's life. "Can't you make negotiations? Why the fighting?"

"They don't want to negotiate. They want to win. It isn't about killing the royal family anymore. It's about taking land."

"Then Sterling should be here with me. Or me with him."

Gilberd shook his head. "This is his duty. He won't hide."

"But he will hide me?" She wanted to pull her hair out at her own frustration. There was only so much to look at within these dreary gray walls. Only so much to do. Each day consisted of cleaning wounds, changing bandages, and saying prayers. She was lonely. And sad. And felt hopeless.

"I'm sorry."

"You always say that," she hissed, but then forced herself to take a deep breath. This wasn't Gilberd's fault. Sterling should never have sent her here to begin with.

When she silently held out her hand, he placed a letter from Sterling into her palm. She opened it, not caring whether the captain read over her shoulder.

Kathleen,

I hope you receive this letter, as the roads are rough, and the skies are dreary. I'm worried about your safety. Please assure me that you are well.

Sterling

"Is this it?" she asked, disappointment in the downturn of her mouth. She lifted her gaze to Gilberd. "My last letter to him was longer. I thought he wanted to correspond."

"Ah," he said before he patted down his pockets and finally pulled out a crumpled envelope. "He wrote it a month ago, but I was unable to deliver it."

In seconds, she ripped the envelope open to find a dirtied and crumpled piece of paper addressed to her.

Dear Kathleen,

I wish I had thought to correspond much earlier through letters. It's easier for me to express myself in writing. My favorite season is autumn. I enjoy the changing colors and the turn of the weather. I do enjoy music, though I can't keep a beat for the life of me, as you likely already know from my terrible dancing.

In my spare time, at least when I had more time to spare, I liked to take the boat out on the lake and fish. Some days, I would simply lie down and take a nap and hope the boat wouldn't overturn in my sleep. I also like to ride horses.

As far as late replies go, would you like to go for a ride with me? I can show you my favorite trails.

Yours, Sterling

Far too late, Kathleen realized a silly smile lay plastered across her face. The moment she realized Gilberd hid a smirk behind his scarf, she scowled at him. "I don't suppose you will be taking me back down the mountain, will you?"

"Not in this weather. The icy trails are just as dangerous as the enemy right now. Three more months, Your Highness. I'm sure the trails will be safer, and perhaps the king will allow you to return."

Remembering the man who had been buried by the snow, who now lay defrosting near the fire, she didn't argue this time as she sat down to write a reply to her husband. Perhaps they might make a friendship out of this yet.

Kathleen glanced at her sketchbook sitting on the small table tucked in the corner of the abbey's kitchen. Tally marks lay in neat rows, counting the days she remained on the summit. Each day fell into the same routine. Morning prayers. Breaking her fast. Stitching up soldiers. Cleaning floors. Cooking supper. More stitching. Nighttime prayers. The similarity of one day to the next made them blend together, and keeping count was the only way to keep track of the month.

Month not *week.*

Three weeks in the abbey had turned into five months which had turned into ten. By now, she reckoned the snow was beginning to or already had melted in Edilann.

A heavy weariness pressed on her shoulders as she scrubbed dish after dish in the soapy water of the sink.

Her hands stiff and raw from the frigid water, she handed each clean dish to another sister to dry, who next handed it to a sister to put away before the next meal.

A stubborn piece of food stuck to a plate, and she scrubbed and scrubbed until at last it came loose. But when she handed the clean dish to the next sister, she noticed the blood streaming from cracks in her hands.

She sighed wearily and dabbed at the freezing-water-induced cracks with a cloth. Shivers ran down her spine and across her arms. No matter how long she remained on the summit, she could never get used to the chill.

Not wanting to get blood in the soapy water, she sat at the table and rested her head on her fist while she stared out at the white scenery just outside. By now, she knew every rock, pine tree, and brick of the abbey by heart.

Another weight crushed her chest. Longing. Hopelessness. Sadness. A part of her knew she had no right to feel this way. Not when soldier after soldier needed her. Not when she was doing so much good here.

But another part of her felt far too small. Unwanted. Unnoticed. Abandoned. Of course, she knew that a marriage to any man might not have been perfect, nor filled with love but rather duty. What she hadn't imagined was to be cast off immediately, sequestered on a mountaintop with the sunshine in her soul dying little by little each day.

She swallowed and sniffed back the tears burning behind her eyes. Not for the first time, she entertained the idea of asking one of the injured soldiers at the abbey to take her back to Edilann. But not only would that risk Sterling's wrath or disappointment, but it would also cast a shadow of unwanted scandal over herself. This marriage was hard enough as it was without ruining her own reputation.

Marriage.

She snorted as she picked up a quill and added another tally mark to her notebook as the sky began to darken. It felt like a sham of a marriage. Despite his insistence for her to stay at the abbey, Sterling had not once visited himself. Not to remind her of his existence. Not to show her that he remembered her either. Neither to consummate the marriage and lay a permanent claim on her.

The ruby on her ring glinted in the waning light as she turned it around on her dry and cracked finger. Edilann law stated they weren't truly married unless the consummation happened. Was Sterling sending her some sort of message? Did he not want her as his wife? Was it only for show? Or perhaps a way to gain the throne while tossing his wife aside in favor of—

With great effort, she shook the thought away. It was far too easy these days to spiral into a whirlwind of depressive thoughts and beliefs. Sterling wouldn't take a mistress, right? And he must care for her to some degree, because his letters to her were sweet and kind and thoughtful. They often made her smile despite the growing cracks in her heart.

"Sister," someone said behind her, making her jump. "You have a visitor."

Kathleen's head darted up to find Gilberd in the doorway. Shadows lingered beneath his eyes. His beard had grown longer. But he still offered her a faint smile. She couldn't stop the hope from lighting in her eyes, but when he ever so slightly shook his head, the hope deflated just as quickly.

Today, she would not be leaving this abbey.

"I brought you something," Gilberd said, and only then did she notice the squirming movement beneath his coat.

A furry head poked out, followed by two shaggy, floppy ears.

She gasped and stood abruptly, rushing toward him. "A puppy!" Immediately, her spirits soared as she took the small dog from him and cradled her—no, him— against her chest and buried her face into incredibly soft brown and white fur. "What breed is he? Does he have a name?"

The captain shrugged. "Some sort of mutt. No one has named him yet."

A smile spread across her face when the puppy licked her chin. "Is he from Sterling?"

"Well, no. He's a gift from my wife. Our dog had puppies. She thought you could use a bit of chaos in your life."

To hide the burn of gratitude in her eyes, she bent to kiss the dog on the top of his head, to which he attempted to lick her again. "I didn't realize your wife knew who I was."

Gilberd gave her a pointed look. "You are the queen. And you are also my charge. Of course, I would talk about you when I see her."

And Sterling's friend, she silently added.

She smiled. *My friend, too.*

Sister Margaret walked into the kitchen, and the moment her gaze landed on the dog, she placed her hands on her hips. "No animals."

The crushing weight on her heart returned at full force, and the devastation must have been visible on her face because Gilberd stepped up to her defense. "The abbey is plenty big enough for a dog. Surely, he won't cause any issues."

"It's not about space. Dogs are loud, and this is a place of worship."

Kathleen stroked the puppy's soft fur with the tips of her fingers, ready to drop a steel gate around her heart to keep herself from despairing at inevitable loneliness.

Gilberd crossed his arms, which made him appear taller and more formidable. "Summit Abbey is still on Edilann land. Kathleen is your queen. Or have you forgotten?"

The woman's mouth opened and closed as she ran the chain of her Mother Divine necklace through her fingers. At last, her jaw set as she stared back at him. "One week."

"Three months."

"One month."

"Two."

Her jaw worked as if a rebuttal lay on the tip of her tongue, but finally she sighed. "Two. No more. But I expect him to be gone by then."

And then the woman left.

"Thank you," Kathleen breathed to Gilberd. She was not accustomed to asserting her authority as queen, especially when she felt like she had no authority. "Though, I won't be here for another two months. Right?"

His lips thinned. "I don't know."

"Gilberd," she said in a strained voice. "Please. You must speak to Sterling. I don't belong here. Just look outside!"

A sister "shh"ed her from across the kitchen. Kathleen grimaced and lowered her voice. "There is no sunlight. The clouds are too thick for it to break through. And it's far too chilly here."

On cue, a shiver raced down her arms. The sweet dog licked her hands as if to chase away the cold.

"It's not my place."

"But he will listen to you." Would he? "He won't listen to me." Though, she had not outright shouted at him through written word despite asking him several times to go home.

"I will try."

The faintest sliver of hope lit her spirit as she stroked the dog's soft fur. "I will name you Bear, because you look like a little bear to me."

His only response was a series of kisses that coaxed out yet another smile.

Gilberd scratched Bear beneath the chin. "In two months if you are still here—"

"—I won't be." She raised her chin defiantly.

"*If*," he emphasized. "I will retrieve him and keep him with my wife until you are ready to take him back. He's yours. And Sterling won't mind."

"Won't he?"

The captain pulled an envelope out of his breast pocket and waved it in the air. "I believe he mentioned something about it in his most recent letter."

A mixture of resentment and eagerness left a strange taste in her mouth as she snatched the letter from him. How could she both hate and adore someone in the same heartbeat?

Balancing the sweet puppy in one arm and the letter in the other, she read.

Kathleen,

The most recent battle was brutal. There were a lot of casualties, and we had to retreat to safer land across the river. The setback has been most discouraging, especially among the troops. I hope to find a way to boost morale, especially when it feels so far out of reach.

I know we have mostly been corresponding with letters, but...I miss you. Is that so strange? I wish to converse in person rather than through written word.

I hope to hear from you soon, though Gilberd told me you would have your hands full with a dog to care for. Let me know what you decide to name it.

With love,
Sterling

Kathleen ran her finger over the words "I miss you" and "with love." He'd never said anything like that thus far. A part of her wondered if it was him or the discouraging setback that had him writing those words.

"You're smiling again," Gilberd commented, making her jump.

Her smile fell immediately. "I am not. And anyway, aren't guards supposed to keep their observations to themselves?"

He shrugged and said nothing more, but the faintest smirk still hid behind his beard. The familiarity in which he treated her was not common for a guard, but she was grateful for it. In a world where friends were scarce in the abbey, she was glad for his small bouts of friendship.

"Come on, little pup," Kathleen cooed at Bear as she exited the kitchen. "Your father is being most infuriating by keeping us stranded here, but I suppose we must write a letter anyway."

Bear yipped excitedly, inciting a laugh from her when he kissed her chin. She took heart in the fact that Gilberd planned to speak to Sterling. Surely, she and her new furry companion would be out of the abbey before the month's end.

Chapter Six

Winter came and went like a forlorn sigh. Once murky roads bloomed alive. Halted trade due to frozen thoroughfares started up again. Everyone in the palace adopted a spring in their step. Yet the war raged on.

And Kathleen was still in those mountains.

Sterling ran a hand over his ragged face, his fingers catching against the stubble growing on his chin. Nearly a year had passed since he had last seen his wife, and much had changed since then. The war, being one. What he believed had been stunted growth within himself broke free, and he had grown over half a foot. He could also grow facial hair. And he didn't at all resemble the boy who had married her in the first place.

He swallowed, the new Adam's apple in his throat bobbing up and down. Even his voice was deeper. What would Kathleen think when they saw one another again? Would she be upset about all of his physical changes? Honestly, he was glad for them. He felt like a man now, and not at all like a boy. But he cared more about what she thought.

After reading Kathleen's newest letter about painting and her gushing excitedly about Bear the dog and his most recent act of puppy terror, he wrote a quick reply. Not much time remained before his unit needed to leave the palace to deal with a small cluster of Armandy soldiers wreaking havoc in the western towns of Edilann. Between fighting on the battlefield and training to fight on the battlefield, he only wished he had more time to write her.

"One more for the road," he whispered to himself as he blotted the ink and folded the paper into an envelope. He missed Kathleen so much. He only wished he could hold her in his arms and seek comfort and reassurance during the horrors of war. He loved every letter he received from her, as they lifted his spirits when all hope seemed to be lost. A permanent tiredness pounded against his soul, but despite it, he forced himself to trudge onward.

His boots squished through mud on his way to the stables, dozens of horses now saddled with soldiers riding on top wearing chainmail and blue cloaks. Horses whinnied and impatiently stamped their hooves, eager to start the journey westward. A soldier named Raimbaut approached with a set of reins in either hand, leading two horses behind him. He handed the reins attached to a black and white steed to him.

"Any messages you would like to pass on?" Raimbaut asked, and then with a teasing grin, he added, "Though, I refuse to pass along a kiss to the lady."

He despised the flush that crept up his neck at the mention of a kiss. His embarrassment had shown itself seldom these days, but where Kathleen was concerned…

"Kiss her and you'll meet an untimely end," he warned and handed over the envelope. He hadn't even kissed her yet himself. "Just make sure you aren't followed. I don't want the enemy learning of her whereabouts." Not again. When the last spy had gleaned the information, he'd been in such a panic. At least until Gilberd had assured him she was still safe at the abbey.

The soldier nodded his head before mounting his horse and galloping away. Mud flew upward with the impact of each hoof on the ground, creating a fresh scent of dirt and grass in the air.

Captain Gilberd approached with a look of uncertainty in his eyes. "May I speak freely, Your Highness?"

"We're friends. You may speak to me as you wish." It didn't matter that the captain was fifteen years his senior. They had grown close in the last year.

Gilberd stroked the nose of his own horse as if gathering his thoughts before speaking. "Do you think it's wise to keep Kathleen at the abbey?"

"She'll be safe there."

His friend shook his head. "The world is never a safe place, no matter where you are. There comes a time when you must live your life and enjoy what you have. I love my wife and children. They could be separated from me at any moment. But being near my beautiful, loving Mirabelle beats any danger we might be in."

Sterling spoke the truth of the uncertainty swirling like black shadows in his heart. "Gilberd, Kathleen was inches away from taking that arrow herself. In the palace. In my own *home*. If I can't protect her when I'm there, I certainly can't do so when I'm gone fighting. She will return when it's safe."

"And what if the war drags on for years? What then?"

"It won't." He ran a hand through hair stiff with dirt, perspiration, and who knew what else. "Just a few more months. That's all."

He'd been saying that for many months now, ever since the day he'd sent Kathleen to Summit Abbey. It had been almost a year. What if his friend was right? But was the risk worth it?

Shaking his head, he decided against it. Just a few more months. Then they could resume their marriage where it had left off.

Chainmail clinked together as he mounted his horse, but when his gaze roamed across the grim faces of his soldiers, he realized something needed to change. A get together. No, a ball. Perhaps a couple of them. He would throw a ball in which they could dance with their sweethearts or woo ladies of the court. He hoped it was enough to revitalize their spirits.

Kicking his horse forward, he took the lead at the front of the line. If any of his soldiers were to fall, he would fall with them.

Two months came and went. On the morning of the last day of the second month, Sister Margaret stood in the doorway of the room she shared with five other sisters, fingers drumming on crossed arms.

"The dog goes."

Kathleen pulled Bear closer where he snuggled with her in the bed. Heartache grew in her chest. Not just from the thought of her dog getting taken away, but from the idea of being alone again. Sterling hadn't allowed her to leave. And now her new best friend would be stripped from her as well.

"Please allow me to keep him longer." *I need him.*

"We made a deal. Two months. No longer." And then the woman left the room.

Each foot dragged as she dressed for the day, keeping Bear close. He'd grown over the past two months, now as tall as her knees. Without him, she didn't know how she could possibly survive more time on the summit.

When Gilberd arrived at the abbey and took the yapping, protesting dog away, she broke down into sobs.

And found herself alone once more.

The second winter in the abbey passed, and Kathleen felt like she had no more tears to weep. When was the last time she'd seen the sun? The pink blush of silky flower petals? A ray of warmth from the heavens?

She held her hands over her mouth to stifle her sobs as she stared down at a plethora of letters. One of her friends from back home would have a baby late spring. Her sister had married three months ago, and she'd only just found out now. Another sister was planning to get married at the beginning of summer. Courtships and marriages and children. Life was going on without her, and she had been stuck in the abbey for nearly two years now.

Unable to live life.

Unable to speak to her sisters, to make friends, to enjoy the small pleasures of life.

Unable to grow a family.

Another sob wracked her frame at the sight of Sterling's latest letter, delivered by both Gilberd and Raimbaut. Because they had come together, she'd been so sure they would take her home this time, but her husband's offending words stared back at her from the page.

The war continues. I look forward to when I can see you again. Hopefully soon.

In the past two years, many soldiers had sought refuge in the abbey, mostly wounded soldiers from Edilann in need of medical attention. Kathleen had helped tend to them, stitching up lacerations, splinting bones, cleaning cuts.

How many times had a soldier tried flirting with her, not knowing of her identity? Remaining true to Sterling was a real struggle of hers, especially when little hope or happiness lifted her spirits. With each passing month, her resentment for her husband grew, brambles and thorns weaving their way around her heart. How less lonely she'd be to slip into a soldier's warm bed or to run away with a handsome stranger to somewhere Sterling would never find her.

The struggle to end her own loneliness by taking a lover and betray her husband was too much to bear some days, so she spent those days rolling bandages instead of being near the wounded men.

But as she read Sterling's letter for the second time, the little hope inside her heart popped like a bubble.

Slowly, she raised her gaze to Gilberd to find true regret in his eyes.

"Take me home. Now."

A dark threat loomed in her voice. She'd never spoken to him like this. But she felt so close to breaking. If she didn't leave the abbey today, she would crumble like a mudslide breaking away from a hill.

The captain swallowed. "You know I can't."

A fiery ache festered in her heart. Loneliness. Abandonment. Neglect. She'd had enough. A priest was scheduled to arrive at the abbey within the next few weeks. Surely, the man would grant her an annulment. She was done with Sterling Winfield after his latest letter. After he had once more broken his promise to allow her to leave the mountain. There was more than one good reason the priest would grant her an annulment. To abandon one's wife, for one. Non-consummation of a marriage, for two. Depriving one's wife the right of children, for three.

A few months of Sterling's absence, she could understand. But nearly two years had passed. She was furious. Heartbroken. Depressed. She deserved better than this.

And by the sullen, pitiful look on Gilberd's face, he seemed to think so as well.

A heartbroken tear escaped her eye. She quickly swiped it away with her palm. Emotion built up inside her, threatening to crumble her to pieces. "Excuse me," she whispered.

Hopelessness, panic, and fury drove her feet forward, slowly at first, and then she picked up her pace until she was running. She threw off her veil, her hair flying free behind her. On her way to the door, she grabbed a cloak and hastily pulled it over her shoulders. Only when Sterling's soldiers seemed to realize what she was about to do did they shout and run after her. But they didn't reach her in time before she slammed the abbey door open and sprinted out into the cold blizzard.

Fierce wind whipped her face, the unforgiving chill nipping at her nose and cheeks. The frigid summit air burned as she breathed it in. But the shouts behind her drove her forward. Snow entered her slippers, but she trekked onward as quickly as she dared, squinting through the mountainous blizzard haze.

She wasn't sure how much time passed. Seconds? Minutes? Her limbs became numb, each step more difficult than the last. The swift wind picked up, grabbing her cloak and seizing her hair. She blindly took the next step forward but didn't have time to cry out as a patch of snow crumbled beneath her weight. For a moment, she fell through a thicket of icy air before landing hard on the ground.

Darkness claimed her, consciousness returning in small windows. She was vaguely aware of being lifted into a pair of arms, and sometime later, she woke just enough to hear muffled voices beside her.

"Should we tell the king?"

A pause.

"She'll recover. No need to worry him."

If her body would obey her, she might have shed a tear. But it was weak, and even her heart didn't have the strength to lift herself from the cot.

Music and laughter lifted into the air of the ballroom, smiles replacing the once grim and hopeless looks of Sterling's soldiers. He had invited not just the nobility of Edilann, but the lower class as well. A cluster of his soldiers stood with a small group of women on one side of the ballroom, effectively wooing them by the smiles and blushes raging across the women's faces.

A pang of sadness entered his heart as he thought of Kathleen. She had never blushed in his presence. If given the chance to woo her, would she eventually come to blush?

He bit his lip as guilt overcame him. Two winters had passed since he had sent her to those mountains. *Two*. He had thought the war would only last a short while, but it continued relentlessly. He'd lost many of his men. Several of the villages within his kingdom had been burned down. No matter how hard they fought, their enemies kept coming. Yet, Kathleen had never written a nasty letter to him, and he hoped to keep it that way. It seemed as if sending gifts with his letters helped appease her.

Just a few more months.

"Your Highness," Lady Whitcomb said as she dipped into a low curtsy, her elderly legs wobbling at the action. She was accompanied by her son, Henry, and her two daughters, Abigail and Emmy. "We wanted to ask after Queen Kathleen. How is she faring?"

"She is faring well. I am hoping we might yet be reunited before the season's end."

"A well-deserved reunion if you ask me," Abigail giggled, who couldn't have been more than fifteen years old. "I reckon she has only grown more beautiful in her absence."

Lady Whitcomb *tsked*. "Stop that, Abigail. You are making our king blush."

How embarrassing... He hoped that someday he might be able to control his blushes that seemed to have a mind of their own.

Thankfully, a familiar, welcome face entered the ballroom. Raimbaut still wore his uniform and chainmail, and in his hand, he carried an envelope.

"Excuse me," he gasped. His rush toward the messenger did not go unnoticed and earned him a couple dozen chuckles from his soldiers, but he didn't care. Kathleen had written him. Nothing was more important to him at the moment.

He snatched the letter out of Raimbaut's hand, broke the humble wax seal, and slid the letter out of the envelope. Beautifully written words were scrawled across the page in Kathleen's handwriting, which never failed to create a bubble of excitement within him.

"Read it out loud!" someone shouted, and Sterling glanced up to find that the ball-goers had created a semi-circle around him, each expression eager to hear from their queen. Music stopped playing, and he was more than aware of everyone's attention on him. Over the last two years, he'd become more confident in himself as a person and as a king, and the attention didn't bother him anymore.

"Fine, but this is the last time." He smiled, smoothing the paper. The letter was dated several days ago, and he noticed the words appeared shaky, unlike her normal careful script.

"That's what you said last time, too," Gilberd grinned, "and the time before that."

Waving away the comment with his hand, he read, "*Sterling, it seems as if the snow has melted in Edilann, as I just received a half dozen of your letters at once. I am joyous* to learn that the war has turned in our favor, and I do hope it remains that way. We have received far too many wounded soldiers here, so my hands have been busy. I have learned a great deal about treating wounds and bringing down fevers. I am quite handy with the needle and have found I excel in stitching lacerations. It seems as if embroidery practice actually pays off.'"

A rumble of laughter moved through the crowd like a brisk wind. He continued, "*It brings me great sorrow to see such hopelessness in their eyes. Healing from a wound can be a daunting task, but I always remind them that they will see their loved ones soon. The reminder often brings smiles to their faces. I pray the war will end soon. Kathleen.*'"

He tried to hide the wave of disappointment within him. This letter had been far less personal than the rest. In the others, it almost seemed as if she had grown fond of him. But he was glad for the letter at all.

More laughter followed him as he exited the ballroom in search of parchment and a quill. He found what he was looking for in his room, sat down, and readied his quill. He wanted to share tonight with her, to share of the joy the ball brought to their people.

My Dear Kathleen,

We have seen our fair share of wounded soldiers here as well. I honor their love and sacrifice for our country. Their grim faces inspired me to host a ball, which I am currently missing as I write this. I think the morale of our soldiers has improved astronomically tonight. They are laughing and dancing and drinking with merriment. The music is nice. It makes me think of you. Spring is now upon us, and every breath I breathe is filled with plumes of pollen. I'm not very fond of it, but I know you are. The rosebuds in the garden have started to grow, and any day they will sprout. I have instructed the gardeners to pay special attention to your roses. I know how much you love them.

I must get back. I am to deliver a toast to our subjects.

All my adoration,
Sterling

Satisfied with the words on the parchment, he sealed the letter into an envelope. But before he left the room, he spotted the rose he'd given Kathleen on their wedding day. He'd saved it and hung it to dry. It now rested on top of a shelf, a permanent reminder of his sweet wife.

He smiled softly as he trailed a careful finger over one of the dried petals. Soon. He would see her very soon.

He left and sought out Raimbaut. The man was deep in conversation with two ladies, and he seemed to be thoroughly enjoying himself. When Sterling approached, Raimbaut rolled his eyes and sighed dramatically.

"I just got back, Your Highness. Will you not allow me a few days to enjoy myself before I must be off on your errands?"

"Fine," Sterling chuckled. "But I expect a hasty delivery when you are well-rested."

The letter wasn't particularly important, so a quick reply wasn't necessary. He simply wanted to hear from Kathleen again. Each of her letters filled him with joy, and he often found himself rereading them from the stack inside his desk drawer. He'd taken them on countless journeys across the kingdom in the past two years. They brought him peace in the midst of war.

He furrowed his brows when he noticed a uniformed soldier approach Gilberd and whisper in his ear. The captain's expression hardened moments before he turned in Sterling's direction and pulled him off to the side as if to avoid being overheard.

"What is it?" His heart raced as his thoughts immediately jumped to Kathleen. Had something happened?

"Armandy is pressing in. They've already taken the plains and are camped out there."

His heart calmed a fraction. Kathleen was safe in the mountains. Their enemies wouldn't know to look for her there.

He nodded, quick with his decision. "We'll ride out with our own army. Gather the troops. We'll push them out of our kingdom and hopefully end this war once and for all."

Chapter Seven

Kathleen stared bleakly out the window, no longer caring about the cold seeping through the glass and wrapping her in a frigid cocoon. Her shawl fell off her shoulders, and no drive remained to secure it around herself once more. She wished the snowy winds would burst into the abbey, only to pull her into its icy grip and disappear with her forever. No existence was much better than this existence.

Her gaze slowly fell to the scrapes on her hands from the fall a week earlier. A part of her wished she'd been left at the bottom of the cliff to die. Getting dragged back to the abbey to live even more of this dreary existence had killed her spirit.

Her spirit didn't fight anymore.

There was nothing left to fight for.

The air stirred when someone entered the room, but she didn't turn her head to see who it was. She simply continued to stare outside, her gaze slowly roaming from one end of the mountain peak to the other. Nothing but snow and rocks and more snow.

"Your Highness," Raimbaut said after a moment. "A letter from the king."

The soldier slid the sealed envelope in front of her. Only after a few long moments did she tear her gaze away from the window. Another letter. More empty promises and a barren field of apologies. He had not once apologized for sending her here. He had not once given her a date of when he planned to retrieve her.

A part of her regretted sending her last letter filled with a bunch of nothingness. But Raimbaut had insisted she write one, even just after waking from her fall. He feared disappointing Sterling far more than she thought was warranted.

Surprisingly, her fingers worked just enough to break the seal and slide the letter out. Each word she read crushed her heart more and more until nothing remained but a pile of broken glass. Life was going on without her. Balls and parties and music and laughter. And she was not a part of it.

Sterling had forgotten her.

He'd needed a wife to keep his kingdom, and now that he was married, he didn't need her anymore. There was no other explanation for leaving her here for nearly two years.

She turned back to the window and watched as snow gathered on the glass panes. Small flakes piled higher and higher until they tipped over the sill, only to start the process again.

"Your Highness?" Raimbaut asked hesitantly. "Would you like me to leave while you write him back?"

Her voice felt raw as it escaped her throat. She was still recovering from her injuries. "No. I will not write a reply. You have no letter to deliver."

"But…but…he will be expecting one."

"Then it is his loss."

"I can't return empty handed."

Finally, she turned her attention to him, only to find worry deep within his eyes. Though, she had no idea if it was worry over her well-being or worry over disappointing his king. Likely the latter.

"There is a box beside the door." Her gaze flickered to the green box latched closed. "Take it to him, and you will not be empty handed."

Relief filled his expression, at least until he unlatched the box to look inside, and his face blanched. "What is this?" he whispered.

"Every gift Sterling has ever given me. Return it to him."

He shook his head and closed the lid with a bang. "I'd rather return empty handed."

She turned back to the window, hiding the tears leaking from the corners of her eyes as she turned her ruby wedding ring around and around on her finger. Treating the wounded soldiers had kept her busy, and doing something worthwhile had helped ease the burden on her heart. She would keep doing good here, with or without Sterling. At least until she could figure out what to do next.

With as much authority as she could muster, she said, "Your *queen* ordered you to take the box to him. Will you disobey an order?"

For a moment, he didn't answer, and she didn't dare turn her head to look his way when tears still ran freely down her face. "No, Your Majesty," he finally said meekly. "What would you like me to tell him?"

She turned the ring around her finger one last time, slipped it off, and placed it on the edge of the table. Raimbaut's breath hitched before tentative steps approached. Finally, she heard the slide of metal against wood as he scooped the piece of jewelry up.

"Nothing. Let him come to his own conclusions."

Something scraped off the floor, followed by the opening and closing of a door. Only when she was certain she was alone again did she turn her head toward the door. The box was gone, and so was Raimbaut.

She buried her face in her hands and sobbed. Two years! Her friends were all having children. Her sisters were getting married. Twenty-two was old enough to be considered a spinster. The priest had accepted her request to meet with him next week, and she was confident he would allow an annulment.

She had waited for Sterling. And waited. And waited. If she got an annulment, who would have her now? She wouldn't be good enough to make another quality match, even one of her own choosing. Sterling had ruined her by leaving her in this blasted abbey. She wanted to leave.

But where would she go?

As Kathleen had expected, another messenger, one who was not Gilberd or Raimbaut, arrived promptly a few days later. The messenger stood in the doorway, eyes searching, and she stared more intently at the stitches she pulled in and out of a soldier's arm. Her hands shook, still recovering from her previous injuries, but the stitches were still decent quality. With hunched shoulders, she tied off the last stitch and fumbled to clean her needle. Would the messenger notice her amongst the other sisters?

"Your Highness," the messenger said, gently touching her elbow.

Drat.

"What is it?" She avoided his gaze as she moved to the next soldier, the man's leg twisted at an awkward angle. He was unconscious, thank goodness for that.

With gentle movements, she straightened his leg and frowned at how loose the joint felt in her hands. The knee seemed to be dislocated. It would take two of them to snap it back into the socket. Reckoning that the soldier didn't wake too early and fight back.

"A letter from His Highness. He will have you read it immediately."

Despite her heart pounding with nerves, she maintained a neutral expression and motioned to another sister for help. "You can tell *His Highness* that if he wishes to speak to me, he can do so in person."

"He cannot. He is locked in battle."

Together, she and another sister counted to three. While the sister held the man's thigh steady, Kathleen snapped the joint back into the socket. The soldier grunted, but otherwise didn't wake. Poor soldier. What must he have gone through?

"I am busy."

"Please, Your Highness. It's urgent, he says."

Taking a deep breath through her nose and letting it out slowly through her mouth, she took the letter from him and opened it. Sterling's handwriting was messier than usual, as if he had been in a hurry to write it.

Kathleen,

I received the box of gifts I have given you over the past two years. Were they not to your liking? I can send something different. What would you like? Anything you want, it's yours.

Sterling

She snorted a very unladylike snort. This letter was urgent? A part of him must at least realize something was amiss. "How dense can you be?" she murmured. Raimbaut seemed to have caught onto her meaning immediately, and the letter was clear enough for her to understand that he had avoided telling Sterling what it meant. Coward. Raimbaut was a coward. Even if she had told him to tell Sterling nothing and allow him to come to his own conclusions.

Allowing another sister to take her place for a few minutes, she located parchment and ink to form her reply, though she didn't take as much care with her letters. If he wouldn't, then she refused to as well. Formal greeting, yes. Formal ending, double yes. Signing her maiden name, triple yes.

Your Highness,

I apologize for not returning your correspondence. I did not wish to. Let me explain what it means for me to return your gifts and the ring. It means that my interests are better left elsewhere. I am angry with you. Here you are, telling me of the wonderful happenings of a ball, of music, of laughter, of merriment, of life going on without me, and then you send me useless gifts I cannot wear because they are too gaudy and not at all simple enough to be seen in an abbey.

I wish we had never married. This new lonely existence is heartbreaking. There is no laughter here. We must speak in whispers, anything louder is promptly hushed. Snow falls from the skies day in and day out, no matter the season. The walls become grayer with each passing minute. I dress in black and white. The walls are black and white. The skies are black and white. I loathe it here. It is an existence that would only welcome death by the hands of our enemies should I have stayed.

I ask that you stop sending me gifts. Jewels and finery are not allowed, despite my station. I also ask that you cease writing to me altogether. My heart cannot bear it. I will only say this once. I have waited, Sterling, far longer than I should have. The very least you could have done if you wanted to keep me was to come up here yourself and consummate the marriage. You are a coward.

I am done waiting. A priest is here at the abbey. I am going to ask for an annulment. You have ruined me, Sterling.

Do you understand? No one will have me now. But it is better than being stranded in these mountains.

Kathleen de Clare

The bitterness of two long years of loneliness clung to the page. Before she could take back her response, she sealed it in an envelope, handed it back to the messenger, and dismissed him. Not waiting to see his reaction, she returned to the wounded soldiers and got back to work, all while trying to snuff out the resentment rising within her.

The flames of her anger refused to die. In fact, they only grew larger like an uncontainable wildfire. War or not, Sterling should never have sent her to these mountains.

CHAPTER EIGHT

The week in the encampment felt like an eternity. The fighting raged on and on and on, with no end in sight. Sterling returned from each battle completely worn thin, barely hanging onto the edge of alertness by the end of the day. He needed more sleep. And a bath. When was the last time he'd taken a bath?

He and his soldiers sat round the fire, the flames casting shadows across the clearing. His gaze traveled to the sky, at the beautiful stars and half-moon overhead. What was the sky like where Kathleen was? Could she see the stars? Could she feel summer just around the corner? Her roses were likely starting to bloom by now.

His heart rate picked up when he heard clomping hooves, followed by the emergence of a familiar face astride a horse. The messenger hopped down from the creature, and after a quick search, he approached him with a letter in his hands.

"From Her Highness," he said before bowing away.

Sterling couldn't open the letter fast enough. He wanted to please Kathleen, but it seemed as if he may have missed the mark with the gifts he'd given. What would she like instead? Soft slippers? Dried roses? A bottle of sunlight? He'd do anything for her, give anything to her.

"Don't leave us in the dark!" a soldier shouted, and everyone's attention snapped in Sterling's direction. "What does the letter say?"

With a snort, he moved closer to the fire for the light to illuminate Kathleen's words. He cleared his throat and read, "*Your Highness, I apologize for not returning your correspondence. I did not wish to.*"

His heart froze, his tongue ceasing to work. Ice crawled through his bloodstream as he continued reading the letter silently, and the more he read, the colder he became despite his proximity to the fire. He ran a hand down his face, once, twice.

Angry? Lonely existence? Coward?

Finally, his heart plummeted to his toes as he traced the word *annulment*. True, they had not consummated the marriage. The law stated they weren't truly married if it didn't happen. She likely would have no trouble getting an annulment if she desired it.

"What?" he whispered, still in shock. All her letters to him had sounded so pleasant. Where had this come from? Had he missed something? An annulment went far beyond the reach of mere anger or annoyance. She must despise him enough to go as far as that.

He lifted his gaze to find everyone staring at him, but he did not wish to explain the contents of the letter. What was he to do? They couldn't get an annulment. He cared for Kathleen. Could she not see as much?

"Gilberd, Raimbaut," he said, motioning for them to follow him. Only when the three of them were out of earshot beneath a cluster of trees did he turn on them. "Have the two of you been keeping things from me? I have only sent a small handful of trusted messengers to see Kathleen, but you two have seen her the most." He loved Kathleen. Each letter she'd sent him had him falling harder and harder for the woman he'd married almost two years prior. He couldn't lose her. His voice cracked with emotion. "Have you left things out of your reports?"

Gilberd shuffled his feet as if uncomfortable. He didn't meet Sterling's gaze. "Every time I went, she begged me to take her back to the palace. She…cried a lot. I don't think she is very happy."

His heart sank with dread. He hadn't known…

"And Raimbaut?" he asked in a hoarse whisper.

Raimbaut frowned and crossed his arms over his chest, glancing once at Gilberd before meeting his eye.

"During the last visit, she tried to travel down the mountain by herself in slippers and a thin cloak. She didn't get very far when she slipped off a small cliff. She was injured in the fall. Badly scraped up. A head injury that left her unconscious for a time."

Fury raced through his veins, and he wanted to throttle his men. "Why did you not tell me?"

"I tried multiple times to convince you to bring her back," Gilberd answered. "But you were so preoccupied with the war and with her safety, you wouldn't listen."

The blood rushed from his face as he recalled each instance when the captain had tried to convince him to bring Kathleen back. He'd thought it was a matter of opinion. Not that his wife was unhappy.

"You should have told me she was injured," he seethed at Raimbaut. "I sent her there for her safety. That does not sound like safe to me."

"My apologies," Raimbaut murmured. "She recovered quickly. We didn't think it was a big deal to worry you."

"It *was* a big deal!" he cried, pointing to the letter. But when a handful of his soldiers glanced their way, he lowered his voice. "Kathleen wants an annulment. And. I. Did. Not. See. It. Coming. The priest is already at the abbey. I don't know how long I have to convince her against it."

"She can't get an annulment. The marriage has already been consummated."

Sterling ran a hand down his face, realizing his trail of mistakes. The boy had married her, and the man was going to lose her.

"Oh," Raimbaut mumbled. "I forgot you sent her away on your wedding day. I didn't realize… This isn't good."

"No, it's not. What am I to do?" He paced back and forth and stopped suddenly. "I'll go up there myself, with a whole carriage full of roses if I have to. I'll leave right now." He turned on his heel, but Gilberd squeezed his shoulder with a strong hand.

The captain's mouth turned into a frown. "The roads are dangerous, especially for a lone traveler. Raimbaut and I take great care when we travel to Summit Abbey. You cannot go alone. You will need soldiers at your side."

With a nod, he released the tense breath festering in his lungs. The panic. The heartache. The need to hurry. "What else do you recommend?"

"Six soldiers. Keep it small as to not attract unwanted attention. The mountain passes are difficult to traverse. We'll send a carriage for her and hide it in the trees at the bottom of the mountain, and then a soldier will ride up to fetch her and bring her back down. You and the remaining five soldiers will be waiting to escort her a little way down the road."

"But what if she refuses to come? I need her consent. I need it before we do any of this." Because her lack of consent to send her there in the first place put him in danger of losing her. He didn't want to do that again.

Raimbaut stepped forward. "I will go ahead of time and tell her of the plan, and when I return with her written consent, then we will act."

Sterling walked quickly to his tent, the other two trailing behind him. He would explain everything in a letter. He would beg for her to give him another chance. Somehow, he'd make things right.

When he sat down to write it, Gilberd ruffed up his hair. "She's not going to recognize you."

"Yes, she will. I don't look that much different."

His friend snorted. "You literally grew a head taller. You are capable of growing facial hair. And you are much bulkier than the scrawny kid who married her two years ago."

"Kathleen will know it's me. There has to be some similarities she would recognize."

"Let's take a bet, shall we? If she doesn't realize it's you, then you owe me six silver pieces."

"You have yourself a deal."

CHAPTER NINE

Raimbaut made an appearance only a few days later, and Kathleen ignored him as she knelt with the other sisters in prayer. When she had first started praying with them after arriving, her knees had ached with unbearable pain. But now they didn't hurt anymore. Even two hours into prayer. Many of the other sisters had already left to tend to the wounded soldiers, but for Kathleen, praying to the Mother Divine eased the pain in her heart.

An annulment… What had she been thinking? It was bold of her to demand such a thing of Sterling. Her anger had gotten the best of her. She should have allowed her anger to dampen before writing the letter. They could have talked about their relationship. They could have spoken to each other instead of her running to a hasty decision.

Of course, she still wanted an annulment over staying at the abbey. But she could have brought it up in a nicer way, or at least have talked to him.

"Your Highness," Raimbaut said quietly, lightly touching her shoulder. "Forgive my intrusion. I must speak with you."

"We have nothing to discuss." She ignored the growing pressure of nerves tumbling in her stomach and instead listened to the hushed whispers of the sisters in prayer.

"I have a letter from Sterling. He wants to retrieve you immediately."

A gasp escaped her lips. Her eyes flew open. She spun around to stare at Raimbaut with wide eyes, but there was no jest in his expression. Her heart pounded in her ribcage, but she dared not hope. Hoping only led to disappointment. "Are you in earnest?"

He nodded. "Come with me and we will discuss more."

She tripped on her skirt in her haste to stand, and he barely caught her by the arm. He led her into another room, a small fire trickling in the hearth and two sisters conversing on one side. When he produced an envelope, her heart squeezed uncomfortably. How would Sterling respond to her last letter? Would he be angry?

With shaking hands, she opened the letter.

Kathleen,

My heart is heavy as I write this. I had no idea you were so unhappy. Gilberd and Raimbaut left some very important information out of their reports, and I am beyond upset. I do not want to use my men as an excuse for your unhappiness. This is my fault, not theirs. For you to have risked death just to get off that mountain...

Why did you not tell me? All of your letters seemed as if all was fine. I am your husband. I want to be your friend and more. I don't want an annulment, and I will do everything in my power to convince you otherwise.

But first, I need to get you off the summit. Then we can worry about everything else later. I want you to pack your things. As soon as I have your permission and the go ahead from Raimbaut, I will send a soldier to retrieve you. More soldiers will be waiting at the bottom of the mountain to escort you to safety. We must do this quickly. The roads are dangerous. If you can wait, at the most, a week, then I promise you will never have to step foot in the abbey again.

Kathleen, please give me another chance. I want to make this right. I beg you not to stay and seek out the priest. We can talk about this, and if you decide you still want the annulment, then I will comply. But I care about you. Immensely. I want you to know that.

Please reply with haste. I am eager to see you. Our reunion has been long overdue.

With love,
Sterling

Tears escaped her eyes after reading the letter, and still after reading it once more. She clutched the letter to her heart, allowing his words to mend some of the hurt and the resentment that had gathered over the years. If he was willing to try to make this work, then so was she.

Finally, she wiped her tears with the back of her hand and nodded. "If Sterling will allow me to leave, then I will go."

Raimbaut pushed a parchment and quill in her direction. "I need your written consent."

She sat at the table and penned a letter to Sterling, not caring that Raimbaut watched over her shoulder. The quill scratched against the parchment, quick in her haste. Despite herself, she felt the smallest stirrings of hope within her.

Sterling,

This is more than I had hoped for. Thank you. I will be ready for your soldier. I don't have many things, as I sent most of what I owned back to you. If you promise that I never have to cover my hair again, then I won't seek out an annulment. But if you break your promise to me...

Please remain true to your word.

Kathleen

The part about covering her hair was a jest, the first bout of humor she'd felt in a long time, likely even since Bear was taken from her. Just the thought of leaving the abbey filled her with so much joy. Bits and pieces of herself she had lost started to come together once more. She dared not give into the pull of hope. If Sterling broke his promise, it would crush her until nothing remained.

She handed the letter to Raimbaut, not bothering to seal it. "Please hurry," she whispered. "I'm not sure how much longer I can stand it here."

Giving her a contagious smile, he nodded his head. "For you, my queen, I will move as swift as the wind."

She watched his retreating back until he disappeared, and with a spring in her step, she hurried to pack her things. Even if it took them days to get to her, she wanted to be ready.

Kathleen watched the front door day in and day out, behavior which turned into obsession. She made it a point to pass it at all hours of the day. She'd even snuck out of bed a few times at night just to look out the window. Still no soldier. But she refused to give into despair. Sterling had asked for a week, so she would give it.

The day before the week was up, the front door opened to reveal a tall man wearing chainmail. He didn't appear to be injured, and the bronze pin on his cloak...

Excitement churned within her as she recognized the symbol on the pin—two crossed halberds surrounded by a laurel wreath. He was from Edilann.

She disappeared for a few minutes to change out of the habit and veil and into the dress she had arrived in two years ago. Blood no longer stained the bodice, as she had thoroughly washed it. Several times. There had been a lot of blood.

Despite having nothing more to wear than dainty slippers and a cloak, she rushed back out with a small bag in tow. A smile beamed across her face as she said goodbye to the sisters and kissed each of their cheeks. Although she would miss them, she would not miss this abbey.

"You're wearing that?" the man said with a grimace. "It's much too cold outside."

"I don't care *how* cold it is. Escort me down. Now."

The soldier's mouth twitched in amusement, but he otherwise said nothing as he opened the abbey doors. A fierce, freezing wind blasted into her face, but she found herself smiling against it. Freedom... Only a little while longer.

He helped her onto a horse before swinging his leg over and sitting behind her. Even this close to him, he kept his distance, only touching her once to place her hands on the saddle to hold on. The choppy ride through the snow and fierce wind nearly made her fall a couple of times, but raw determination had her fingers and legs latching on tighter. The tips of her ears and nose froze, and she found breathing difficult as the minutes passed into what felt like hours.

Dark green pines covered in snow. Rocks nearly buried beneath the white powder. Gray and alabaster skies that eventually ceased releasing its snowflakes.

At last, the snow thinned more and more with each step. Her heart nearly burst inside her when she spotted green. A plant! Oh, heavens, it was a plant. Not just a pine tree. But an actual plant that needed more sunlight than snow.

She might have cried if the wind wasn't trying to freeze the moisture in her eyes.

Little by little, the wind died down, the snow dispersed until only patches remained, and she began to feel her face again. Instead of snow, dirt and grass stretched across the ground. Instead of snow-covered pines dotting the landscape, stunning green leaves and shrubs took their place. Beautiful, flowery aromas greeted her nose—a nostalgic smell she hadn't had the pleasure of experiencing for too long now.

But before she could admire the scenery for long, the soldier stopped his horse and helped her down. A lone carriage waited within the confines of the trees, which he quickly attached the horse to.

"Best get inside," he said, motioning with his head toward the carriage. "We still have about an hour's ride until we reach our party."

Although she did as he asked, she kept the window open. A flutter of excitement turned her stomach when the carriage jolted forward. The leaves on the trees became a brighter green with each passing minute. And the sky! Oh, the sky! It was blue. Very blue. With adorable puffy clouds drifting past. The number of snow patches decreased until they disappeared entirely.

And then she saw them.

Flowers.

Beautiful, colorful, magnificent flowers.

A delighted giggle escaped her as she leaned precariously out the window to snatch blooms as they drove past, until her hands were filled with petals in an array of colors ranging from red to pink to white to yellow. She tucked the flowers into her hair and wove them together by the stems to create a bracelet.

The carriage rolled to a stop. Despite what danger might await on the roads, she wasted no time as she burst out of the door, laughing as she twirled in several large circles with her arms outstretched. "Oh, it's so beautiful! I have not seen a flower in years. And the sky! Would you just look—"

She froze, her smile falling and her eyes wide as she beheld a group on the road ahead. Men. Six of them.

She gasped and ducked behind the carriage, her back to the smooth wood. Her breaths became shallow, filled with fear. Bandits. They were bandits. She didn't have anything on her person but flowers, as she had given her crown and ring back to Sterling with the rest of his gifts. Would they kill her? Capture her for ransom?

No, no, no. She couldn't die. Not like this.

"I apologize," someone with a deep voice called out. "We did not mean to frighten you."

Her heart still beat faster than a hummingbird's wings, but she dared to peek her head around the side of the carriage. The six men didn't move in her direction. They stood still, as if waiting for something.

The man who had spoken stood in the middle of the road, flanked on one side by three men, and on the other by two. All wearing Edilann uniforms. She sighed in relief when she recognized one of the men—Captain Gilberd.

Thanks heavens. This is my escort.

Pushing away from the carriage and rounding the corner, she approached timidly. Her heart beat quickly for an entirely different reason as she stared at the man in the middle, the one who appeared to be the leader because he stood at the front. He was the one who had called out to her. He was handsome. Very handsome. His messy brown hair swept over his forehead. His blue eyes shone as brightly as the sky overhead. The lines in his jaw stood out on his face.

Her gaze involuntarily roamed over his broad shoulders, across his armor-covered chest, and she couldn't help but notice how tall he was.

Guilt slammed into her stomach. She was a married woman, yet she had ogled him as if she hadn't seen a man in two years.

An involuntary blush stole across her cheeks. With a swallow, she asked, "Who are you?"

The five men flanking him burst into laughter, and the man in the middle let out a huff before turning to place a sack of coins into Gilberd's hands.

When he turned back to her, his mouth turned upward in a half-smile. A familiar half-smile. Where had she seen it before?

"I don't know whether to be offended or amused that you don't recognize your own husband."

Kathleen's lips parted in surprise, and she allowed her gaze to roam across him once more. The hair color and eye color were the same. The smile. But everything else...

Her mouth dried at having to look *up* at him and not *down*.

"Sterling?" she breathed, which earned another round of laughter from the soldiers. "But you're...but you're..." She didn't know how to finish the sentence. Handsome? Gorgeous? Breathtaking? Tall? *Different?* How could one person change so much in the span of two years?

He grinned, and her heart nearly melted where she stood. "And you're..."

A laugh escaped her, more from shock than anything. It was as if her feet moved on their own accord as she took a step forward, and then another, before she flew into him, her arms wrapped securely around his waist. He was solid against her. Even his arms were much bigger than she remembered as he hesitated for only a moment before wrapping them around her shoulders.

Relief swelled within her, though she wasn't sure if it stemmed from seeing him again or from simply being out of the abbey. All of the letters they had written to one another came flooding back to her mind. To her heart. Warmth. Friendship. Familiarity.

Her husband.

"Look at you!" she exclaimed, holding him at arm's length and this time shamelessly perusing him with her gaze. "You're not a boy anymore."

More guffawing from the soldiers.

Sterling rolled his eyes good-naturedly. "That's just what every man wants to hear from his wife..." he muttered.

Her smile blossomed as she glanced down at her feet. Quietly to herself, she added, "I can wear heels again."

His arm stiffened against her hand, and she lifted her gaze to find his expression serious from the hardness of his eyes to the jumping of his jaw. "Then does that mean you…"

He didn't finish the sentence. It seemed as if they were both unable to speak clearly. She was still flustered from the shock of coming home to find a completely different man from the boy she had left. Why *he* was flustered, she didn't know.

Very suddenly, he breathed in sharply and pulled her closer to him, followed by a *thunk, thunk*. Lifting her gaze, she found that Sterling had lifted a shield above their heads. Two arrows protruded out of the wood.

War cries. Everywhere. Men ran out of the trees with their weapons drawn, and Sterling's soldiers rushed forward to meet them with their own swords. These weren't bandits, no. They were Armandy soldiers.

Real, genuine fear slammed into her. Her heart jumped to her throat. Her legs became wobbly. The clash of steel against steel rang in her ears, nearly drowning out the sound of Sterling's voice.

"Hold them off!" he ordered in the voice of a king. "I'll get her to safety."

Two strong arms lifted her into a saddle before they wrapped securely around her waist. The horse jerked forward at Sterling's kick, and faster than she thought possible, their surroundings flew by in a dizzying whirr of green and brown.

Pounding hoofbeats sounded from behind, a soldier in pursuit.

She wanted to cry. They were going to die.

Sterling twisted in the saddle with a crossbow in one hand. *Clink! Whizz! Thunk! Grunt. Thud.*

The bolt seemed to have hit its mark, but she didn't dare turn to look. She clung to the saddle with a grip so tight her fingers turned white. His hold around her waist tightened, and the horse galloped even faster.

She didn't know how long they galloped for. It could have been minutes. It could have been hours. But when they burst into a war camp lined with tents and filled with hundreds of soldiers, the horse finally slowed to a jerky trot and then came to a full stop.

"Are you all right?" Sterling asked in her ear. "Are you hurt?"

When her voice refused to cooperate, she shook her head. She was not all right, she was not hurt.

He dismounted the horse first and placed his hands on her waist to help her down, but when her wobbly legs nearly collapsed beneath her, she latched onto the saddle to keep from falling.

Worry creased the space between his eyebrows, something she had found adorable when they'd first married. But she couldn't appreciate it as much as she wanted to when shock tangled in her limbs and shook her to the core.

After helping her sit on a log, he paced back and forth, his nervousness transparent in his expression as he kept looking toward the road. She watched him pace once more before he moved to his horse as if to mount, but before he placed his foot in the stirrup, pounding hooves sounded down the road. Six horses, a carriage, and six soldiers rode into camp, everyone seemingly unharmed. But she had seen plenty of battle wounds firsthand. Those soldiers could possibly be badly bruised beneath their armor.

"What happened?" Sterling asked, and Captain Gilberd answered.

"We were ready for the ambush. I'm just glad you got the queen out in time. We defeated most of the men. The rest fled."

Now that her legs were strong enough and didn't threaten to collapse on her, she stood and started to trudge away past a row of gawking soldiers and toward a thicket of trees. Her shock wore off, her fear slowly disappearing as all of her emotions came tumbling down at once—relief, shock, resentment, anger. Unfortunately, anger was the strongest.

"Wait, Kathleen," Sterling said as he grabbed her hand.

She yanked her hand out of his grip, turned sharply, and slapped him across the face. The sound reverberated through the camp. Every conversation hushed immediately, and all eyes turned in their direction.

"That was for sending me away for *two years* on our *wedding day!*" she cried.

Shock filled his eyes, his fingers grazing his raw cheek. The red print of her slap began to form on his skin, but she was too upset to feel guilty about it.

Tears streamed down her face, an unstoppable flood. She cradled her hands to her heart. "Did you forget about me?"

"No," he replied hurriedly. "Not at all."

"Did you just need a quick wife in order to keep your throne, and I happened to be available?"

"No, Kathleen." His voice was thick with husky emotion. "It wasn't safe."

She continued as if he hadn't spoken, her tears falling even faster. "I feel like you abandoned me."

"No. I swear on my life it was never my intention."

She furiously wiped away her tears and gestured to the camp around them. "Why did you retrieve me? It's obviously still *not safe.*"

"Because you sounded so upset in your letter."

"No." She balled her hands into fists at her sides, trying to keep her temper in check to keep from pounding on his armored chest to release two years' worth of stress, worry, anger, and resentment. "You sent me away because you were afraid to lose me. You retrieved me because you were *afraid to lose me*. You can't hide the things you want under a rock and expect to keep them!"

Her voice bordered on the edge of hysterics. Every harbored emotion tumbled out, disorienting when she didn't know exactly what she should be feeling. So many things. Nothing made sense in the fog of confusion in her heart.

He stared at her as if stunned, and an awkward silence descended upon the camp. Everyone still watched them as if unable to tear their attention away, but Kathleen didn't care. She was too angry to care.

"Are you going to say anything?" she asked when his silence stretched for too long.

"What do you want me to say?"

Gilberd hissed between his teeth and murmured, "Wrong answer. He'll be sleeping outside tonight."

"Well then," she replied quietly, her eyes as cold as the blizzards on the summit. "I should thank you for retrieving me from the mountain, but since you put me there in the first place, I feel as if you do not deserve thanks."

Without another word, she walked away and found a quiet place behind a tree to gather her thoughts and emotions. There were far too many to sort through.

Chapter Ten

Ouch. Sterling felt her rejection like an arrow to the heart. Or a slap to the face. Oh wait, that already happened...

He brushed the tender skin on his cheek and watched as Kathleen pointedly ignored him. She sat beside the growing fire with a sketchbook and ignored all his men, too, while she sketched.

He took several steps to the right, and sure enough, she adjusted in her seat to keep her back to him at all times. She was aware of exactly where he was. The sting of her rejection flamed hotter.

How humiliating... Two years of separation had nearly made him forget about her temper, as well as her delight in public humiliation when she was upset enough. Of course, he didn't think she had intentionally humiliated him in front of his men, but it would have been nice if she had been just a little more discreet.

"I thought she would be happy to leave the abbey," he muttered as he slumped down next to Gilberd where he sharpened his sword. Of course, Kathleen turned at an awkward angle to face away from him a little further away. "She seemed happy to see me at first. And now this? I don't understand."

Gilberd chuckled, dragging the whetstone across his blade in repetitive movements. "Welcome to being a man. Understanding the way women think is a lifelong process." His gaze briefly flickered to Kathleen. "Never go to bed angry, I always say. You should talk to her."

"And say what? She is furious with me." He glanced up at the sky and noticed the position of the sun sitting just above the mountain range. He dreaded the coming nightfall. Would his wife make him sleep outside the tent? Or perhaps she would choose to sleep with the other female nurses near the medical tent.

Either option would be terribly embarrassing for him.

"I think she wants you to apologize. What else could she have wanted you to say at the end of your lovers' squabble?"

"Apologize for what? I did what I thought was best for her."

"And you didn't give her a choice in the matter. Do you remember what she said to you before you sent her away? She begged you to let her stay. You didn't listen."

"I did what was best for her. I have nothing to apologize for."

Gilberd sighed and shook his head disappointedly. "I have been married for many years, Sterling. I remember standing where you are standing right now. Sometimes we are prideful in our decisions. But you must be careful not to take your pride to your grave. Marriage is not about being *right*. It's about love and compromise. She is hurting because she feels unloved and abandoned. If you can't apologize for your actions, then at least apologize for the way you made her feel."

He ran his hand down his face, acknowledging the truth to his friend's words. When it came to marriage—and honestly, women—he was very inexperienced. "She won't listen. She'll shout at me again."

"Maybe. But are you going to allow her to keep feeling the way she does? It's worth a try at the very least."

With a nod, he wrung his hands in nervousness as he glanced at Kathleen, noting the rigid posture of her back and the tight grip on her sketchbook. "I have an idea. Do you think the soldiers are up for a little exploration through the forest?"

I slapped a king.

Kathleen nervously tapped her drawing utensil on her sketchpad, trying not to hunch her shoulders when she felt more than a few stares on her back. Would Sterling punish her? He hadn't done anything thus far. He hadn't so much as spoken a single word to her since their fight.

Once again, her temper had taken control, and regret seeped into her conscience. How could she look her husband in the eye again? What had she done?

Her thoughts occupied most of her attention, allowing her hand to sketch as if on its own accord. A rose. The very one Sterling had given her on their wedding day. What had happened to it? Had a servant thrown it away? Or was it dry and brittle where she had left it in the vase in her room at the castle?

A surprising ache settled in her heart at the thought.

A real, tangible purple wildflower fell onto her sketchbook. Her head snapped up to find a smiling soldier, a man with graying hair who appeared to be at least fifteen years older than Gilberd.

"For my queen," he murmured before backing away.

She set her sketchbook aside and furrowed her eyebrows in confusion. Giving her a flower was a very kind thing for him to have done. Had she looked dispirited enough to warrant the gift?

Another soldier bowed before her, one who looked about as young as Sterling when they had first met. He offered her a yellow wildflower. "For my queen."

What?

When a third soldier approached, she tentatively got to her feet and took his flower as well, one with beautiful violet petals.

Tears sprang to her eyes when one by one, soldiers handed her flower after flower, adding an array of color to her bouquet. Emotion gripped her heart, squeezing it so much that she thought she might start weeping with gratitude at any moment.

For so long, she had felt unseen, unwanted, and abandoned. Lonely. Sad. Unimportant. But these simple gifts of natural beauty? They meant more to her than all the clothing and jewels and finery in the world.

Raimbaut and Gilberd offered her a flower, and then Sterling stepped forward with his own cluster of pink evening primroses. More than that, her wedding ring held the bunch of flowers together. A silent question. A hopeful offering.

A blush dusted across her cheeks as she gazed back into his blue eyes, the color barely visible in the light of dusk. He didn't hand the flowers to her. Not yet.

"I should have taken more care to listen to what you wanted, to what you needed. I never intended for you to feel hurt or abandoned. Kathleen, will you accept my apology?" He lowered his voice, his expression pleading. "Will you forgive me?"

At last, her pool of tears escaped and ran down her cheeks. She wanted to forgive him. She truly did. But her heart hurt too much. How could she trust him again? What if another war broke out in the future and he sent her away a second time? What if they had children and he did the same to them? Her heart couldn't bear it.

Her gaze lowered to her feet. "Forgiveness isn't so easy."

Several beats of silence, and she dared to glance up to find torturous regret in his eyes.

"Then will you accept my promise? I promise to never send you away again, and especially not without your input." He swallowed, his thumb gently caressing the ruby ring. "Please give me another chance."

Sincerity lay within the depths of his eyes. He spoke with genuineness, with promise. She remembered his sweet, thoughtful spirit, his oblivious but hopeful nature. And as she gazed back at him, *up* at him, she couldn't help but take in his handsome, heart-melting features. *Handsome*, not cute anymore. His physical changes gave her incentive as well, as much as she hated to admit it. But could they rebuild the trust broken between them? Could they overcome this huge obstacle in their path?

She gave him a watery smile. "I am willing to try again if you will forgive me for slapping you."

"It did sting a little," he teased, his lopsided grin creating butterflies within her stomach. She still couldn't get over how much his physical appearance had changed. She could stare into his eyes all day.

"It probably hurt my hand more than your face," she laughed, wiping her cheeks with her palm.

"Then it's settled? We've reached a truce?"

She reached for the cluster of primroses in his hand, and a jolt of excitement rushed through her when their fingers brushed. As she added them to her bouquet, she smiled into the flowers and inhaled a deep breath of the sweet, wild aroma. "You certainly know the way to my heart, Sterling Winfield. I cannot resist beautiful flowers." She slipped the ring back onto her finger, the ruby glinting in the firelight. "A truce it is."

Soldiers whooped around them, and she joined in with her own joyous laugh. However, her smile faltered into surprise when Sterling took her hand and brought it to his lips. Heat traveled from her fingers, up her arm, and claimed her face as a deep blush flamed in her cheeks.

"You're blushing," he grinned, his voice lost in the chatter surrounding them on all sides.

Quickly, she tried to mask her fluster by bringing the bouquet of flowers to her nose. "I am not."

"You are. I had hoped I might someday be able to make you blush. It makes me happier than you realize." He stepped closer to her, and she stared intently at a particularly delicate pink blossom to avoid looking at him. "I don't remember you being so short."

She cursed her lack of control as her gaze shot up to meet his. *Up,* not *down.* Again, she delighted in that fact alone. "I don't remember you being so tall."

Her heart pattered in an uneven rhythm when he took her hand, and she felt as if she walked on a cloud as he led her to an unoccupied log away from earshot of the other soldiers. They sat, almost close enough for their knees to touch.

Her stomach fluttered when he trailed a finger down a strand of her hair, and she was grateful not for the first time that she no longer had to hide it under a black and white veil.

"I don't remember you being so beautiful."

Where was a fan when she needed one? Her fluster catapulted to the clouds drifting lazily across the darkening sky overhead. Was he flirting with her? This was very unlike the stuttering, unconfident Sterling she had first met. But unlike back then, he no longer felt like a stranger after sending dozens upon dozens of letters to one another.

Could she flirt back? Was a bouquet of flowers really enough to make up for two years of misery?

There *were* a lot of flowers. At least one for each month of her seclusion. And she *did* love flowers…

Unfortunately, it was not enough. She needed him to demonstrate to her that he could take care of her heart instead of lock it away in isolation. But she had promised to give this a try.

With newfound confidence, she met his gaze and gave him a coy smile. "I remember thinking you were cute when we married. I don't remember you being so handsome."

"Cute?" He laughed, the rich timber of his voice sending chills of exhilaration up her spine. "Should I take offense to that?"

She counted on her fingers. "Short, scrawny, inexperienced, boyish. But cute. And sweet."

His smile never disappeared, and she was glad he didn't seem to take offense to her honesty. "It was all worth it just to see your shock at our reunion. You know, I was the only one who bet you'd recognize me. It turned out I was wrong."

"Can you blame me?" She nudged him gently with her elbow, and he nudged back. Neither of them moved away from the faint touch of their arms.

They were silent for a few moments, and she found her gaze traveling to the fire where a pot hung over the flames. One of the soldiers started handing out bowls of stew, first to her and Sterling, and then he continued down the line.

Although ravenous with hunger after so long of fasting, she ate slowly, savoring the flavorful venison in each bite.

Sterling's voice broke into her thoughts. "The abbey couldn't have been all bad. Was there nothing you enjoyed there?"

"There were a few things." Using her spoon, she stirred her stew absently. "I loved the sisters there. They felt like family after a time, though Sister Margaret was far too strict for my liking. Stitching up battle wounds and fixing soldiers' injuries was satisfying as well." She glanced at him to find him grimacing, and she nudged him playfully. "Don't give me that look, Sterling. It took a couple of weeks until I stopped being squeamish enough to approach a bloodied soldier."

"Should I be envious of any of the soldiers you came across?" Real concern rested on his brows, as if the thought had kept him up at night on more than one occasion. "I am not beyond issuing a beheading."

Though his tone suggested a jest, uncertainty leaked through his voice. It reminded her of the Sterling she had met two years ago.

She placed a thoughtful finger to her lips. "There was one male, in particular, I had grown fond of. He was very hairy, his kisses a bit wet, but enjoyable all the same. He shared my bed for a couple of months." She watched in amusement as he clenched his fists. "Oh, and he was my dog, Bear. I only wished he could have stayed longer than two months."

"Kathleen," he breathed, squeezing his eyes shut. "Don't do that. I was ready to run a man through with my sword."

"Truly?" She cocked her head to the side, studying him. "You would duel a man in the name of my honor?"

"Yes."

"Why?"

He picked up a nearby stick and dragged the tip through the dirt. For a moment, she thought he wouldn't answer, but when he did, he didn't meet her gaze. "Is a husband not allowed to grow fond of his wife?"

"Aside from our correspondence, I've had more conversations with Captain Gilberd than I have with you. You couldn't possibly be fond of me."

"I was fond of you long before we got married."

"Oh." She tucked her hair behind her ear and preoccupied herself with arranging the flower bouquet and rearranging it just to keep her hands busy. She wasn't sure what to make of his confession. The first time she met him had been when she arrived in Edilann. Right? She couldn't recall meeting him before then. But could she be wrong?

Thankfully, Sterling redirected the subject to their earlier conversation, excusing her from replying. "Let me guess what you hated the most about the abbey. Covering your hair."

"Oh my heavens, yes. Those veils were dreadful."

He laughed, still drawing in the dirt. "I can only imagine."

Someone cleared their throat, bowing low before addressing Sterling. "Your Highness, where would you like us to put Queen Kathleen's trunk full of the things her ladies maid sent?"

Mauve? Oh, bless that woman! Kathleen was in desperate need of a change of clothes.

"Umm…" He bit his lip, casting a sideways glance at her. "I…umm…where are the nurses sleeping—?"

"Place them inside Sterling's tent," she interrupted as she stood, and only when the soldier left did she roll her eyes. "Please, Sterling. We are married. Don't embarrass me."

She followed the soldier to a large white tent facing east, only to find Gilberd and Raimbaut moving their own things out. A new nervous rhythm pounded in her heart at the thought of sharing a tent with Sterling. Alone together. What would that be like?

Resisting the urge to roll her eyes, she entered the moment everyone else left. Sharing a tent with Sterling would be uneventful if his hesitancy only a minute earlier proved anything. She had wondered if he would have been brave enough to consummate their marriage on their wedding night. She hadn't gotten the chance to find out. But despite his flirtation earlier, she still doubted anything would happen tonight.

The tent stood tall enough for her to stand and walk around. A single lantern illuminated the several trunks that lay on one side of the tent, next to a neat row of weapons and armor. On the other side of the tent lay a single bedroll, large enough to comfortably fit two people.

A wicked smile spread across her face. How would Sterling react to a little teasing?

Although she had not yet forgiven him, she had decided to give him a chance. Consummating the marriage would take away her chance to get an annulment, but she didn't want an annulment. Not anymore. Not when she could see a promise of a hopeful future ahead of her.

Brushing her mischievous ideas aside, she opened her own trunk and sighed in relief, silently thanking Mauve for packing all the essentials. A couple of gowns, including a nightgown. A sturdy pair of shoes capable of withstanding the woodsy wilderness. And her favorite, a few canvases and an easel, accompanied by paint and brushes. Her ladies maid never disappointed.

She changed into her nightgown, and she just finished lacing the front when Sterling stepped into the tent. His eyes immediately widened, and he inhaled a sharp breath of surprise. "Oh, sorry." He turned away from her and stared up at the ceiling. "I'll just…um…I…"

"Oh my, Sterling. I am beginning to wonder if you realize you knelt at an altar by my side."

"Sorry," he murmured again. A flush crawled up his neck and turned the tips of his ears red. He slowly lowered his gaze from the ceiling and looked her in the eye. Or he at least tried to and failed. The bodice of the nightgown dipped low, laced in the front by a ribbon, the white fabric dripping to her feet.

She smirked, watching his stunned reaction as she slowly pulled on one side of the tie, loosening it enough to tease, but not enough to reveal anything. "It was easy enough to put on. I suppose it would be just as easy to take off."

He simply stared, his flush growing brighter by the second.

After a few moments too long, she huffed and re-tied the lace. She wasn't sure what she was more embarrassed by—Sterling's inability to play along, or putting herself on a thin layer of ice, only to fall through into the cold, icy lake of rejection. Of course, Sterling wasn't ready for this. She shouldn't have tried. She briefly wondered if she had thrown herself at him, if he would have been ignorant of that hint as well.

"What is wrong with you?" she growled, angrily stuffing her day dress back into her trunk. "I'm sure most men would have jumped at that invitation."

"What? That was an invitation?"

"Not anymore."

He shook his head and took a couple of steps toward her, but she didn't look up as she added her slippers to the trunk beside her dress. "Let's start again."

"I'm no longer in the mood." Her feet were already icy as it was, and her bravery had fled. She didn't want to fall completely through the frozen lake should he find another way to reject her advances.

"That quickly?"

"That quickly," she affirmed. Her gaze traveled to the bedroll on the ground, and she truly wondered if Sterling had meant all of his promises he'd made to her. Perhaps it was not kind to test his willingness to make her happy now, but her embarrassment still lingered in the flush in her neck. "I ask that you find me other sleeping arrangements."

A look of uncertainty passed across his features, and if she dared to think it, perhaps a small sliver of embarrassment, too. "What would others think?"

"Your pride be darned. Find me another bedroll, Sterling."

Several moments of silence. He released a terse breath and pinched the bridge of his nose. "I have enough pride to not go begging around for my own wife to sleep apart from me. Have my bedroll. I will sleep without."

Her heart skipped in surprise. He hadn't suggested she sleep with the nurses. He hadn't stormed out to find another tent to lay his head. And even more importantly, he didn't suggest she return to the castle for her "safety".

At last, she exhaled. "I simply wanted to find out how you would react to the suggestion. I'm more than happy to share the bedroll with you."

He gave her an incredulous look, to which she returned with an eyebrow raised in a challenge. "You just said—"

"You were willing to make accommodations. That's all I really wanted."

Scratching his head, he trudged toward the bedroll and laid down, a deep weariness visible throughout every inch of his body from his exhausted eyes to the slump in his shoulders. "Are all women like this?"

"Yes." She blew out the lantern, plunging the tent into darkness. A mumble of low conversations and laughter from the soldiers echoed outside, muffled by the tent standing between them.

Weariness pressed down on her own shoulders, and overly aware of her quick-beating heart, she climbed into the bedroll beside Sterling, making sure not to touch him. The heat his body gave off beckoned her closer like an alluring invitation, but she refrained from giving into the pull.

She stared up at the tent ceiling, wide awake despite the exhaustion of many sleepless nights at the abbey and a long, jarring journey down from the summit. It felt surreal to be beside her husband again, and she reckoned adjusting to his presence would be no easy feat.

"I think we need to talk about the letter you sent me," he said suddenly, breaking the silence. "I don't want this hanging between us."

Of course. The letter… "What about it?"

He shifted until he turned toward her. Despite feeling his gaze on her, she continued to stare at the ceiling. "If you were so unhappy at the abbey, why didn't you tell me?"

She picked at the corner of the bedroll to occupy her hands. "Because I thought you already knew how miserable I was. I didn't realize your messengers were keeping you in the dark. Hence why I became so resentful toward you."

"Ah." A long pause. "I know I shouldn't be…but I am furious with them. They didn't even tell me you had fallen off a cliff! Tell me what happened."

With a shrug, she breathed in slowly and let it out even slower. "No one would escort me down the mountain, so I tried to leave by myself. In the blizzard, I didn't see the drop-off. I don't really remember falling. I woke up a couple of days later to find myself back at the abbey."

"That scenario could have ended up vastly different, Kathleen. You could have died. You could have been captured by the enemy. You could have been eaten by wolves."

"I know," she whispered. "But loneliness was a worser fate."

When he didn't reply, she turned around to face him, only to inhale sharply when her hand brushed against skin. She snatched her hand away immediately, but the heat of him still lingered in her fingers. "Are you unclothed?"

"Only halfway. I get hot at night. Do you want me to put my shirt back on?"

"N-n-no." Ah! Now who was the stuttering one? "It just surprised me is all."

More silence, and although she closed her eyes and attempted to sleep, it jumped just out of reach. She opened her eyes again only to find him staring at the ceiling with regret in the pinch of his mouth.

As if feeling her gaze on him, he turned his head slightly to look at her. "I'm not sure I can sleep."

"Me neither." Especially not when faced with the hard, muscular planes of his chest. No, definitely not scrawny anymore. A desire to touch him surfaced, and she only wished she could take back his suggestion that they start over in their attempt to consummate the marriage. Perhaps *she* was the one not quite ready yet. Her heart needed more time.

Sterling turned on his side, his head resting on his hand as he gazed down at her. She swallowed the thick tension in her throat as she stared back into his eyes. Too much space rested between them. Far too much space.

Kiss me, she thought, but didn't say the words out loud. She couldn't even clear her mind enough to give him a hint that she wanted it.

"I hate that you were lonely," he whispered huskily. "I feel so…oblivious. I didn't think. I just didn't…" He stopped, his swallow audible in the darkness. "I thought your safety was enough."

In the end, she couldn't stop herself from touching him. It was only a light, feathery touch on the tip of her fingers over his chest. A hint. A reassurance. She didn't know this time. She needed his presence, his strength, his comfort to fill the empty spaces of her heart.

In a whisper, she said, "I don't feel quite so lonely anymore."

Yet, he didn't kiss her. He simply froze beneath her light touch, not even breathing as if afraid to scare her off.

She dropped her hand, once again listening to the hum of conversation outside the tent. The stacking of bowls. The splashing of water. And then she began to shiver when she finally noticed the night's chill descending upon the camp.

"Are you all right?" Sterling asked.

Kathleen rubbed her hands up and down her arms. "I don't know how you can be hot. It's freezing."

Her heart stopped beating for a moment when he wrapped his arm around her waist and pulled her closer to him until she was pressed against his chest. His heat seeped into her, calming the nighttime chill beginning to set into her bones. The soapy, minty aroma of his skin invited her closer, and she couldn't help but breathe him in. Her head spun, excitement and nervousness churning within her stomach.

"How is this?" he murmured.

"Good," she squeaked, and cringed at her own voice. At least she hadn't stuttered. "Very warm."

"You're really that cold? It's spring."

"Have you no experience with women? We are always cold. No matter the season."

He chuckled. "How did you survive the snowy mountains?"

"I hardly did. Hence my outright hatred of you. Out of all the gifts you could have given me, you should have sent an eternal flame."

Another rumble of amusement in his chest. "There is no such thing."

"How disappointing. It would have been nice."

When he spoke again, his breathy voice caressed her ear. "Do you still wish we had never married?"

"Don't…" She released a delighted, shuddering breath. "Don't ask me like that. You have an advantage when I'm unable to think clearly."

His chest rumbled with laughter. "That wasn't my intention. I take it as a 'no' then?"

The hope in his voice made her smile. "I like seeing you work hard to earn my favor. Ask me again tomorrow."

"I plan on it. And every day after if necessary." And then gooseflesh raised on her arms as he trailed his fingers from her wrist to her elbow. "Do you still hate me?"

"No," she breathed. A pause. "My hands are cold. I think you should warm them, too."

A pleasant shiver raced up her spine as he intertwined his fingers with hers. Finger to finger. Palm to palm. Their faces were so close. She felt each one of his breaths on her nose. If she tipped her head up, she could easily touch her lips to his. But she couldn't, no matter how much she wanted to feel his kiss. She needed him to take the initiative for this.

Yet, he didn't.

More silence. A comfortable silence. She knew the man beside her. They had written letters back and forth to each other for two years. Despite all the resentment and the anger and the frustration, she considered him her friend.

"Are you sure you're not in the mood?" he asked suddenly.

"Goodnight, Sterling."

She smiled against him and nuzzled closer to his chest. A friend, indeed. But perhaps something more as well.

Chapter Eleven

Sterling blocked Gilberd's swing with his sword, the clash of metal on metal echoing in his ears. They traded blows, each quite evenly matched. He was overly conscious of his footwork—one of his sword-fighting weaknesses. Not to mention the fact that it was extremely difficult to keep his gaze from wandering toward the edge of the training field where Kathleen sat at a small table, sketching in her notebook. Her beauty distracted him and being distracted during a fight was *not* a good thing.

Gilberd fell for Sterling's feint attack, and far too easily, Sterling unarmed his opponent and pressed the tip of his sword close to his neck. "What are you doing?" He frowned and lowered the point of his sword. "You are never defeated so easily."

The captain grinned. "I'm trying to make you look good in front of your wife."

He laughed and stooped down to pick up his friend's weapon before handing it back to him. "Then I'm afraid you must do it again. I don't think she was watching."

"Are you sure? She's watching right now."

Involuntarily, he turned his head in Kathleen's direction, and his heart ceased beating when he found her looking right at him. A smile blossomed across her face as she gave him a dainty wave. He still couldn't believe it. That was his *wife*. Somehow in the past two years, she had grown even more beautiful. She may have covered her hair the entire time, but the soft, silky strands still had a sheen to them as if she hadn't missed a day in the sunlight. And her eyes... Her intense blue gaze captivated him and made his mouth dry each time he looked into them.

"Sterling? Hello? I'm still here." Gilberd snapped his attention away from her. "You better hope she never finds her way onto the battlefield. You'd be hewn down immediately in your daze of distraction."

"That's why I have you." He grinned as they sheathed their swords and ladled themselves water from the bucket near the weapons tent. "To protect your king on the battlefield, even with your own life."

"Ha-ha, Sterling." The captain gave Sterling's shoulder a good shove. "If I end up dying because of my king's stupidity, I will curse you from the afterlife."

They both slumped into a couple of chairs, exhausted from the morning's training exercises. What he wouldn't give for a warm bath and the comfort of his own bed. Bathing in the river simply didn't compare. And now that Kathleen was here, he reckoned he'd have to bathe more often. He didn't want to smell.

He kicked his feet up on the circular table in front of him, but he almost fell backward in his chair when Kathleen approached while hugging her sketchpad close to her chest, a smile on her lips. His feet came down from the table with a *thud*. His heart thundered in his ears as he searched for something to say, but she beat him to it.

"Good morning, Sterling. Gilberd. It's such a lovely day, don't you think? I woke up to sunlight. *Sunlight*. I don't remember the last time that happened. It's strange to think I missed the smell of earth and leaves. It's something you don't notice when you go about every day."

Upon gazing into her eyes, his mouth dried as if swabbed with cotton. She stood against the backdrop of lush green grass, blue skies, emerald trees, and golden sunlight at her back. Her hair shimmered beneath its warm rays.

He cleared his throat. "I suppose the smell of mud is nice." Gilberd coughed beside him, but he caught the underlying snicker at its heart. He wanted to punch his friend. "What are you drawing?"

She flipped her sketchbook around to show her latest creation. His eyes widened in surprise. While he'd expected to find weapons or fighting soldiers, he instead found himself gazing back at a horse. Gilberd's horse, Eterial. The lines sketched onto the paper accurately depicted the horse's brawny muscles, its long black mane flowing over one shoulder. The image was intricate and accurate down to the fine details such as individual tail hairs. She was a very talented artist.

"I am lacking for words," he said, rubbing a hand down his chin. "You are very…skilled. It's incredible."

What else lay within her sketchbook? "May I see others?"

Kathleen bit her lip and glanced toward Gilberd, but the captain faced away from them, preoccupied with cleaning his dagger with a semi-clean cloth. Finally, she nodded and handed it over. "Don't you dare laugh at me, Sterling Winfield. Or I may never speak to you again."

His mouth twitched. "I don't doubt it. You gave me quite a dry spell last evening before supper."

"You deserved it."

"Probably, yes."

He flipped to the next page to find the detailed image of a dog with big eyes and floppy ears. "Is this Bear?" She nodded. "I haven't met him yet, but I enjoyed your tales of mischief and woe. Sister Margaret about burst a vein—"

"—when he tore up her pillow and scattered the feathers all over her room." She laughed, her eyes sparkling with what seemed to be a happy memory. "You remembered from my letter."

With a shrug, he lowered his gaze as a sudden bout of timidity overcame him. "I remember everything in your letters. I reread them often."

He peeked at her to find her tucking a strand of hair behind her ear and smiling.

Gilberd broke the momentary silence, startling them both as he pointed to the sketchbook. "Bear is even bigger now. I suppose my wife accidentally gave you the biggest of the litter."

Kathleen giggled and rolled her eyes. "You are supposed to be looking the other way."

The guardsman grinned and scooted his chair several feet away. "I'm not here."

Sterling smiled himself at the easy friendship between the two as he flipped over the next several pages depicting different women wearing habits and veils, likely at the abbey. More pages were filled with dozens upon dozens of trees, flowers, and animals. As if she hadn't wanted to forget them during her stay on the summit. A pang of guilt turned his stomach, not for the first time. He didn't regret sending her there, as he feared something might have happened when he'd left for war. But he deeply regretted her loneliness and unhappiness. Perhaps there was something more he could have done to help.

When he turned another page, his breath caught in his lungs. Kathleen tried to snatch the sketchbook away, but he held it out of reach. On the paper lay an incredibly detailed sketch of himself on their wedding day. Sitting in a kitchen chair. His arm bandaged. Torturous fear rested in his eyes.

"This is how you remembered me," he murmured. "What a ghastly sight." He ran a hand over his face. "That arrow hit my right shoulder. If you had turned even an inch, it could have pierced your heart."

"But it didn't."

"But it could have."

She took the sketchbook back from him and turned the page to Bear once again. "Instead of dwelling on could-have-beens, why don't you think of all the mischief you have to look forward to. He's a really naughty dog. I love it."

Laughter burst out of him, effectively dispelling the previous dark cloud hanging over his heart. "I look forward to meeting him."

"What is that?" she asked suddenly, staring right at him. Or past him?

"What is what?" He looked behind him, only to find the pale material of a tent.

A laugh slipped out of her mouth. "It's stubble." She touched his cheek and dragged her fingers across his jaw, brushing his lips with her fingertips. Her hand was so soft against his skin… "It looks good on you."

After giving him a final smile, she continued on her way. He couldn't help but stare after her with a slack jaw. Swishing skirts and swaying hair and grace in every footstep. His heart pounded in his chest. Every fiber in his body thrummed alive at her simple yet affectionate touch.

"Did something happen last night?" Gilberd grinned mischievously, scooting his chair back to its previous position.

Sterling rolled his eyes and punched his friend in the shoulder, earning him a satisfying grunt of pain. "No. We just talked. Not that it's any of your business."

"She is not at all subtle. She wants you to kiss her."

"Really?" He frowned as he gave his friend an incredulous look. "Am I blind then? Or just stupid? I don't catch her hints until it's too late and she gets angry." He remembered one of the first instances on their wedding day when she had been trying to get him to ask her to dance. Now he wanted to go back through all her letters just to see if he'd missed a "not-so-subtle hint" about her being unhappy at the abbey.

"Just stupid," Gilberd laughed, and Sterling shoved him. "I don't reckon you've had much experience with women. It takes practice."

With a weary grunt, he kicked his legs onto the table once more and leaned back in the chair with his arms folded, eyes closed. He felt like he could sleep the entire day. Or week. Maybe even month.

"Well?" Gilberd asked.

"Well, what?"

"Are you going to kiss her?"

"Right now?"

"She asked you to, didn't she?"

He peeked one eye open. "Not now. I need to think of how to approach it. I often freeze around her, so if I'm not prepared, I will mess it up."

Gilberd kicked his legs onto the table as well. "You can't keep waiting for the perfect moment. Snag her heart while you still can. Knowing what I do about her thus far, her gates will snap closed without a moment's notice."

An involuntary groan escaped him, and he squeezed his eyes shut even tighter. "Why can't I be like you? You seem to know what you're doing. Me, on the other hand... I am embarrassed for myself."

"It can't be that bad."

"Oh yes, it can."

He recalled last night and the glaring, embarrassingly obvious hint he'd missed. Now that he thought about it, he wasn't entirely sure how he could have missed it. What else could she have been hinting at? She had practically started to undress in front of him. How stupid was he?

He groaned again and hid his face in the crook of his elbow.

You are a coward. Kathleen's letter came to mind, and he frowned. She was right. He'd had two years to permanently bind them in marriage. His messengers had made it to the summit there and back without too much incident. Surely, he could have found the time as well.

I will no longer be a coward.

But as he thought of how to romance Kathleen in this war camp with dozens of soldiers looking on, he started to drift off, and he didn't realize he'd fallen asleep until Gilberd smacked his arm. He jolted upright.

"Look at that," Gilberd chuckled. "Do you reckon she's gonna try?"

He followed his gaze and watched in amusement as Kathleen dragged her fingers along the racks of bows at the far end of the training grounds. He hissed through his teeth as she picked up a rather large bow almost twice her size. Quietly, he said, "No, Kathleen. Not that one."

His friend laughed, though not loud enough to draw her attention their way. "She won't be able to pull the string back."

Their gazes remained fixed on her as she watched for a minute as the other archers practiced. Nock the arrow. Position the bow upright. Pull the string back. Aim. Release. *Thud.*

She located a quiver of arrows and struggled to nock the first one. She pulled the string back, but when she did, the arrow drifted sideways, away from the bow. She tilted the bow so the arrow returned to the correct position. When she pulled back and released, the bow caught on the fletching, sending the arrow spinning instead of shooting straight. The arrow plopped onto the ground.

He grimaced.

On her second attempt, she nocked the arrow with the fletching facing the wrong way once more. This time, she didn't even get the chance to pull the string back before the arrow wandered away from the bow and plopped onto the ground.

Never mind the large bow. She couldn't even nock the arrow correctly enough to shoot straight.

"Are you going to put her out of her misery?" Gilberd asked.

"No, I'm going to put *us* out of *our* misery. I can't keep watching this." He stood and stepped onto the training grounds. He glanced once at Kathleen, his gaze roaming from the back of her head to her heels. Yes, the second-to-smallest bow would fit her well.

He grabbed a bow the right size for her, tested its flexibility, and then approached her from behind.

Just as Kathleen tried to pull the bowstring back again, something tapped the bottom of her weapon, another bow knocking with hers as if in greeting.

Her head snapped up, and she found herself face to face with Sterling. She couldn't stop the defensiveness that rose to her eyes, the argument waiting on the tip of her tongue. So what if she was a woman? If he planned to stop her, then—

"Shooting a bow is a good skill for a queen to know," he said, and her expression transitioned from caution to surprise. "However, it might help if you learned on a bow that's not two sizes too big for you. This one is better."

When he traded bows with her, her eyes widened further in surprise. Not only would he allow her to shoot, but he would teach her? Sterling was nothing like many of the men she had met throughout her life. She liked that. A lot.

Heat nestled into her cheeks when he stood behind her, her back against his chest. He reached around her with one hand on the handle of the bow, the other holding an arrow.

"Now, when you nock the arrow, you want to make sure this feather is perpendicular to the string," he started to explain, his fingers lightly brushing the tip of the feather. "You don't want to put it on backward and have it catch on the bow when you let it loose."

She found it difficult to focus on his words when his heat seeped into her back. And his hands... They were strong. Capable. Sturdy.

"—pull back the string more to either make the arrow fly a greater distance, or to put strength behind the shot for the tip to sink farther into the target. Are you with me?"

"Mhmm." Oh, his *voice*. Deep, yet soft. It caressed her ear like a lovely, golden melody.

"Place your hand here." He firmly took her left hand and wrapped it around the bow's handle, covering it with his own. His touch left her a bit weak in the knees. "And with this hand, nock the arrow. There you go. Now here's the tricky part. You'll want to keep the arrow steady with the tip of your finger. Lightly rest it on top, that way it won't wander away."

She could think of a few places she wanted to wander away with Sterling...

"Pull it back, keep your arm straight, and line up your shot at eye level."

Although she attempted to do as he instructed, she couldn't pull the string back very far without her arms shaking. When she released the arrow, it flew straight, but dipped down quickly and stuck fast to the ground. It hadn't even made it halfway to the target.

He reached into the quiver and pulled out another arrow. "That was good. You just need to pull the string back a little more." After nocking the arrow and with his hands covering hers again, he pulled back on the string.

Her eyes widened at how much farther he was able to pull back the string than she was. Her gaze traveled from his hands, to his strong, muscular arms. Heat flashed across her body as she listened to the breath that escaped him when he released the string. The arrow flew straighter than a needle toward the target.

Thunk!

It found its mark in the wood.

"Oh my," she whispered. Where was a fan when she needed something to cool her face?

She turned her head to look at him, only for her heart to leap to her throat to find him closer than she'd anticipated. His intense gaze captivated her, shook her soul to the core. Breath fled her as her gaze traced his prominent jawline shadowed with stubble, his adorable ears poking out of his messy brown hair, his long eyelashes framing gorgeous blue eyes, his soft-looking lips curving up the slightest bit on one side.

Oh my... she said again, this time in her head. If she spent another second in his presence, she feared her wobbly legs would collapse on her. Gorgeous? Yes. Masculine? Yes. Strong and capable? Yes. Heart melter? He certainly was doing a good job at that, too.

When she found herself staring, a blush stained her cheeks, and she broke eye contact with him, turning her attention toward the ground. To her surprise, his hand gently cupped her cheek and lifted her head. He moved closer, dipped his head, and brushed his lips across hers in the most tender of caresses. The drums of excitement pounded in her stomach, rose to her heart, and escaped as a hot, breathy exhale. Heat flared alive within her, shooting up her arms like bursts of embers. When he attempted to break the kiss, she wrapped her arms around his neck and pulled him down more forcefully.

Forget the two years in the abbey. Every moment had been worth it. Just for this.

She peppered his lips with kisses, tightening her hold around his neck. Every fiber of her being broke down and rebuilt itself into something completely foreign but beautiful. Like the first breath of spring air. Like a fire billowing on a beautiful night. Like—

Whoops and hollers echoed around them, and they broke apart. Her cheeks flamed hotter when she found that soldiers had witnessed their first kiss like an audience at a knights' tournament. If only they were alone, then she didn't think they'd ever end the kiss.

She was queen, wasn't she? Couldn't she just order the entire camp to leave so she could spend time alone with Sterling?

It seemed as if he had the same idea, as he leaned closer as if to avoid someone overhearing him. His eyes shone with a bright, lively happiness, with a tinge of mischief. "Is a little privacy too much to ask for?"

"Is there such thing as privacy for a king?" She laughed and flirtatiously placed her hand on his hip, looking up at him from beneath her lashes. Oh, yes. He was handsome, and she couldn't keep her mind from wandering as she thought about the feel of his arms around her.

"I'm sure we can find some if we look hard enough."

Her heart caught in her throat when he smiled down at her, and not for the first time, she admired the way one side of his mouth lifted higher than the other.

More whoops and hollers from the soldiers. Too happy to be completely annoyed at their intrusion, she rolled her eyes and stepped away from him. She doubted they'd get any sliver of privacy until tonight anyway.

They both turned back to face the target, falling into a comfortable routine of archery practice. Not a single one of her arrows made it close to the target, but she didn't mind when she was actually spending much-needed time with her husband. Being by his side was like a breath of fresh, warm air, filled with sunshine and wildflowers and joy.

"You know…" she said with a sly smile. "I think the two years apart was good for us."

He raised an eyebrow as he briefly glanced her way before letting an arrow fly. The tip sank into the wood with practiced precision. "In what way?"

Once again, she needed a fan to cool off. She found it attractive that he knew how to use the weapon, and he was good at it, too. "You were able to grow into your role as king."

"How do you benefit?"

"I didn't have to watch."

Her mouth twitched, giving away her jest. He snorted and gently pushed her shoulder.

"There were a few growing pains," he admitted with a teasing smile.

"Just a few?" Her gaze trailed from his feet to the top of his head, sending him into a fit of chuckles once more.

"Just enough for my wife to not recognize me."

"If you had only given me a few more moments, I would have figured it out."

"Lies, Kathleen. But nice try."

She opened her mouth to continue their banter, only for her breath to hitch when he wrapped his arm around her waist and pulled her close. The scent of his minty soap enveloped her, a scent she had quickly begun to associate with him. A blanket of safety filled her with warmth in his arms. Safe. Warm. Happy. She never wanted this happiness to end.

They leaped away from each other when a stampede of horses rushed into camp, led by Raimbaut. The hardness in the man's expression put her ill at ease, worry churning in her stomach. All kindness and humor in Sterling's expression fell into a serious mask, his once jovial eyes turning dark and commanding. It was as if the sun had been covered, leaving only room for shadows. What kind of horrors had he witnessed on the battlefield? What aches and pains lay buried deep within his heart, deeper than even she could reach?

"Sire." Raimbaut dismounted and smoothed his wild hair before handing a rolled parchment to Sterling. At this angle, she couldn't read what it said, but judging by the varying degrees of darkness that pulled Sterling's mouth into a frown, it couldn't be good.

"Have you seen this with your own eyes?" Sterling asked, rolling the parchment to its original position.

Raimbaut nodded. "Nearly half the troop was killed. Others were taken prisoner. The remainder are holding out, keeping the territory. They sent a plea for reinforcements."

By now, most of the soldiers had gathered round, shifting from antsy foot to antsy foot. Gilberd took the rolled parchment and read it for himself.

Sterling gave the order, speaking loudly and with authority in his voice. "We head out immediately. Saddle the horses. Gather the supplies. Don your armor and weapons. Prepare yourselves for battle, men."

A flurry of activity from clanking metal to scraping blades to whinnying horses burst to life around her, disorienting her for a moment. Her heart jumped into her throat, and she gasped as she turned every which way, only for panic to set in when she couldn't find Sterling.

Finally, she spotted a head of brown hair slip into their tent, and she rushed after him. Her anxiety crushed her with every footstep, memories of their wedding day resurfacing in her mind. Sterling pierced with an arrow. Her new husband sending her away for her safety. The panic of not knowing whether he would live or die.

Not again. Not again!

She flung the tent flap aside, only to find Sterling stuffing provisions into a saddlebag and gathering his armor and weapons.

"Don't you dare leave me again!" she shouted, and he stopped for only a moment to glance up at her before resuming his packing.

"What do you think I've been doing in the two years of our separation, Kathleen? I've gone from one battlefield to the next, leading our soldiers in war. As much as I would like to stay, I cannot."

When her emotions threatened to pull her under, she pressed a fist to her mouth and breathed in deeply through her nose and slowly let it out. The war had involved her at the abbey through plenty of wounded soldiers. She could face this dragon. But it was much more difficult when she cared about the man before her.

A trembling breath escaped her. "This was much easier when I hadn't been aware of what you were doing. Please don't die, Sterling. My heart cannot bear it."

And she meant it. Demanding an annulment had been a terrible mistake. After all their letters, she had grown fond of Sterling. Even more so in the past two days. She didn't want to be apart from him again. She couldn't bear such a long separation one more time.

He ceased his packing and gazed back at her, the tent suddenly feeling far too big and him too far away. The darkness fizzled from his eyes, replaced by a sincere and grateful smile.

"You have always been my reason to keep on living, Kathleen. I fight for you. To bring peace to this kingdom so you might enjoy it."

Guilt pierced a hole straight through her heart. All this time, he'd been fighting for her, and what had she done? Sought out an annulment. How ungrateful could she have been for his sacrifice?

"Allow me to help you with that," she whispered. Before he could protest, she rounded him and worked to slip his chainmail over his head and strap on his armor.

He frowned, annoyance flashing across his eyes. "The only reason I can think of for your knowledge of armor has to come from tending to soldiers at the abbey."

She easily detected the jealousy in his tone.

"You needn't worry." She placed a gentle kiss to his cheek. "There was no one else, Sterling. I swear I was true to you."

Still, his frown remained. "But your letter… The annulment portion… You thought about leaving me. It had to be for someone else. Did you meet someone?"

"I met a lot of people," she said carefully, not wanting to upset him further right before he was to go to war. "I dreamt of loving someone and being loved in return." She tightened the strap at his shoulder and started on the next strap. "I would have settled for a farmer or a carpenter or even a bard if it meant reaching that dream."

"Do you not think you can come to love me?"

Heat flared in her face, and she was grateful she stood behind him so he couldn't see it. Realizing her fingers had stilled, she finished strapping his sword belt around his waist and stepped away to pick up his leather gloves.

"Many soldiers turned up at the abbey," she said quietly, fingering the gloves. "Just when we sent one batch off, another would take their place. Many others died from their wounds. I always prayed none of them would be you." She dared to lift her gaze to find him watching her, a softness in his expression she hadn't expected to find. "I never thought my feelings would be the issue. I was so sure you would never love *me*." Especially after feeling forgotten and abandoned for so long.

He clasped both her hands. "Do you know the first time I saw you?"

When she shook her head, he continued, "It was at your coming out ball. I was sixteen at the time. You were eighteen. I was awestruck at the sound of your laughter, at the graceful way you danced. I overheard Lord Rupert bragging that you were practically engaged to him, that your father would agree to the match. I..." He ran a hand down his face. "Perhaps it was a selfish desire of mine. I spoke to your father before the night's end." He chuckled, red tinging his ears. "I felt like a boy then, but I was so sure of what I wanted, the words came easy. I asked for your hand in marriage. I used my status as heir to a kingdom to persuade him. When I would turn eighteen, you and I would wed. He agreed tentatively, a secret between the two of us, unless he found a better-suited match."

Emotion swelled within her throat as she gazed back into his eyes. "So you didn't marry me just because you needed a wife, and I was the one who happened to be available."

Now she understood why the engagement to Lord Rupert had fallen through. As well as a couple other of her suitors, including Nicholas. Eighteen was still young for a man to marry, but it showed her Sterling hadn't wanted to wait any longer than necessary to join their families, especially with her being two years older. He'd wanted her the moment he came of age.

"No." Once again, he ran a hand over his stubble. "I was too shy to ask you to dance that night, and I was embarrassed by our height difference. I thought I'd grow in a couple of years. Lo and behold…"

She squeezed his hands. "You just needed four years, and not two."

He released a shaky breath. "Four years… That is how long I have been fond of you. And I fell in love with you through your letters. You have my heart, Kathleen. Now it is I who must hope to one day have yours."

Every word tumbling through her mind stilled as heat bubbled from her toes to her fast-paced heart. Words refused to grace her lips as she stared at him, each labored breath causing her chest to constrict.

Sterling loves me. But the question is do I love him?

Not even two weeks had passed since she had demanded an annulment. She did not deserve to utter those words, especially when she wasn't so sure about where her own heart lay. Only yesterday had the dying heart in the long distance between them started beating again. She needed more time to be sure.

Instead of waiting on her answer, he leaned forward to kiss her forehead before reaching past her to grab his sword. "I must go now. Several soldiers are staying behind to guard the camp. I will send a couple of them to escort you back to the palace."

She shook herself out of her shock enough to glare at him. "I am staying right here. So help me, Sterling, I will be here when you return."

He stared at her for a long moment, an argument growing in his eyes. But then he unexpectedly sighed. "I made the mistake once of sending you away against your wishes. I will not do it again. I respect your decision. Please stay safe."

"Come back to me safe and whole."

His mouth twitched in a partial smile, though he didn't agree to her demand. With a heavy heart, she watched as he left the tent, mounted a horse, and led his soldiers away. The camp suddenly felt empty and deserted, like she might be able to hear a single hair of her paintbrush drop if she listened hard enough.

"Please come back to me," she prayed, a fierce ache taking hold of her heart. The thought of never seeing Sterling again made panic race through her veins. She prayed harder.

"Please. I beg you."

Chapter Twelve

Chaos erupted around Sterling as arrows fired, swords clanged, and screams lifted into the skies as army clashed against army. The putrid stench of rotting blood mixed with sweat slammed into him as he gazed out over the battlefield atop his horse. His lungs ached for oxygen. Each labored breath he inhaled stung like pins and needles attacking him from the inside out.

War cries and smashing weapons deafened him, his hearing muffled further through his metal helmet.

He inhaled sharply when his gaze landed on Gilberd, who fought mightily with his sword, his armor speckled with blood. An enemy horseman rode fast in his direction, swinging his mace with the intent to kill.

"Gilberd!" he shouted, but his voice was drowned within the sea of chaos. "Gilberd!"

The captain continued to fight, not hearing his warning.

Without a second thought for himself, he kicked his horse forward into a gallop. The fatigued muscles in his hand found it difficult to hold tight to the reins, the sword in his other hand threatening to slip from his fingers.

Gritting his teeth, he urged the creature faster and intercepted Gilberd's attacker just in time. He stabbed his sword upward at the same moment the soldier's mace struck him. The heavy spiked metal crashed into his armored side, and the collision threw him right off his horse and onto his back.

The impact smashed the breath from his lungs. Darkness engulfed him for mere moments before a blinding pain entered his side. He tried to gasp, but something was blocking air from entering. The darkness over his vision turned into a drone of black dots, the buzz swarming in his ears.

"Get the king to safety!" someone cried, their voice barely audible against the incessant ringing.

Faces appeared above him, breaking through the clouds of black dots in the corners of his eyes. Once again, he attempted to take a breath, but something prevented the action. Black dots swarmed faster. His head burst with agony.

He was barely aware of being lifted, the blue skies passing across his vision before turning white as they entered a tent. His chest ached. His side flamed with pain. The darkness dragged him farther, farther, farther.

All of a sudden, the pressure lifted from his lungs, and he gasped. The moment the air returned to him, the black dots swarmed faster before slowing to a gentle lull.

His soldiers moved around him as they cut off his metal armor, a huge dent in the plackart. He focused on taking deep breaths. Raging agony consumed him when someone pulled up his tunic and touched his side.

"You're injured, Your Majesty," a soldier said. Sterling glanced down at his side to find a nasty purple bruise glaring back at him.

Pain rippled through him as he attempted to shift where he lay. He winced at the same moment the tent flap flew open. Gilberd entered with a sword in one hand and a helmet tucked under his arm. Sweat plastered his hair to his forehead, his cheeks flushed red from exertion. The glare he directed at him made him grimace, which promptly turned into a wince of pain.

"How dare you!" Gilberd shouted, looking absolutely murderous. Several soldiers backed away as if terrified to get between this inevitable squabble. "How dare you take that blow for me."

Sterling sat up straighter—or at least he tried to. "H-how…" He swallowed and tried again. "H-how dare you speak to your king that way."

"Exactly!" he shouted, his face turning crimson with anger. "You are my king. We are supposed to protect *you*. Not the other way around!"

"And w-what…" He grimaced again, tenderly holding his side. "And w-what of friends?"

"I am twice your age."

"S-so?"

This got Gilberd to chuckle, but the expression on his face remained dark and seething. "You are infuriating, sire. Let me take a look at the wound."

The other soldiers moved out of the way while their captain inspected the injury. Sterling focused on taking deep breaths as Gilberd probed at the wound, turned his head each way to look into his eyes, ears, and mouth, and then inspected his head as if searching for any other injuries.

Finally, the man placed his hands on his hips and grimaced. "That is a nasty bruise, though I don't suspect any terrible internal damage. To think that could have been my head… Although I'm furious at you, I thank you for saving my life."

Sterling released a breath and fell backward to stare up at the ceiling of the tent. "You can thank me after this bloody battle ends."

Kathleen dipped her paintbrush in white paint and carefully touched it to the canvas, adding the final highlight to Sterling's hair. Ever since he left for battle a week ago, she could not stop worrying about him. Painting helped ease her anxiety, if only just a small portion.

"Dry quickly now," she whispered to the painting while she cleaned her brush. "I would be thoroughly embarrassed if my husband saw you."

She stepped back with her hands on her hips to admire her work. Two years had passed since she'd picked up a paintbrush, but her work wasn't half bad despite the large gap. She'd taken one of her favorite memories of Sterling from last week and brushed it upon the canvas, a memory of him with his hands grabbing a tree branch above him while talking to Gilberd. He'd looked her way from beneath his arm and cast her a coy smile.

Her heart still misbehaved whenever she brought the memory to the forefront of her mind.

A commotion outside the tent snapped her out of her thoughts. Her heart shot straight to her throat as she burst out of the tent and into the dusk of a young evening to find soldiers riding into the camp on horseback. Some were injured. Others unconscious or dead.

Fear gripped her as she stood on her toes, craning her neck for a glimpse of the man she had missed so very much. With each passing moment of his absence, her anxiety grew. She clutched her hands to her heart, hoping, wishing, praying.

There!

A head of brown hair rounded the corner, riding next to Gilberd. Sterling's gaze frantically jumped about as if he were searching for her, too. The moment their eyes met, he dismounted his horse and ran in her direction. Tears streamed down her cheeks as she met him halfway and threw her arms around his neck.

"You're alive," she sobbed into his shoulder. "I was so worried."

They held each other tight as others rushed around them, both soldiers and nurses seeing to the injured. When Sterling's knees started wobbling, she slipped his arm around her shoulders and helped him toward their tent. Uneasiness squeezed her throat when she noticed the blood matted in his hair, the specks of red across his face. She quickly stripped him of his armor and fetched a bucket of water and a cloth.

"Poor dear," she whispered upon her return.

He lay on the ground, taking deep, weary breaths. He blinked heavily as if trying hard not to succumb to sleep. Shadows lined his eyes, his skin pale.

She carefully cradled his head in her lap, dipped the cloth in the water, and dabbed at the matted blood. The bucket of water quickly became tinted with red. Through her administration, she inspected him, though she found no head wounds that would have warranted the damage. This was someone else's blood.

"That feels nice," he murmured, eyes closed.

Keeping her tears at bay was difficult as she continued to weave her fingers through his hair with one hand, and with the other, she wiped the specks of blood from his face. "I much preferred being spared from the heart-wrenching anxiety of your absence. I bit my fingernails to the nubs, and I like my nails almost as much as I like my hair."

His mouth twitched at her jest, but he still didn't smile.

"I have decided you are not allowed to leave again," she continued. With the tip of her finger, she followed the soft curve of his ear, trailing it along his jaw and to his cheekbone. "I don't think my heart can take it."

Finally, he opened his eyes, the blue intensity capturing her own. "Kathleen… I would have us seal our marriage," he said quietly, haggardness heavy in his expression.

"Oh, Sterling." She traced the dark circles beneath his eyes, the tortured downturn of his lips. "You are too weary to stand. We cannot."

"Please," he whispered, trailing a strand of her hair through his fingers. "I cannot stand the idea of ever losing you. The thought hurts too much. Please, Kathleen."

She hesitated at the pleading in his voice. This was not how she had imagined this happening. A wave of desire and passion perhaps. Or a persuasion of duty. Not deep in the trenches of heartache and misery. But how could she deny him? The solidarity of their union was far overdue, and even though this situation was not ideal, she wanted this, too.

At last, she nodded. "Yes, of course, Sterling."

Their next kiss was one of deep heartache, the burden of the pain shared on both their shoulders. Deep in the throes of their passion, she felt a warm tear drip onto her cheek, and then another. And only afterward did Sterling begin to weep into her neck, his salty tears soaking her skin and hair. His anguish also brought her to tears. She held him in her arms, willing his heart to heal. But he continued weeping until finally, his breathing slowed as he succumbed to exhaustion. He fell into a deep sleep beside her, not waking as she gently stroked his hair with the tips of her fingers.

"What did you experience out there on the battlefield?" she asked, her voice no more than a whisper. He didn't stir.

The intimacy of their passionate embrace had surprised her. It was far more intimate than she'd expected from an encounter full of heartache. A bearing of hearts and souls without a single uttered word.

She lay beside him for a few more minutes, at least until she heard the muffled urgency of nurses across the camp. As much as she wanted to stay here with her husband, she had a duty to help the soldiers in need.

After dressing and smoothing down her hair, she exited the tent. A gloom had fallen over the camp like a thick, overbearing fog. Some soldiers wept. Others sniffled or moaned in pain. And many stared ahead with blank expressions, as if their minds were temporarily broken. She'd seen it all too often at the abbey. Broken soldiers. Would Sterling become one of them?

On her way to the nurses' station, she noticed a familiar figure standing with his back against a tree, his arms folded across his chest as he stared toward the fire in the middle of the camp. Gilberd briefly looked her way as she approached before returning his gaze to the fire as if seeing something she didn't. As if reliving the horrors experienced on the battlefield.

She swallowed. "Gilberd, was the battle horrible?"

He released a long, slow breath. "It was like any other. We defeated our enemies and sent the rest running for the hills."

"Will Sterling be alright?" She wrung her hands as she glanced worriedly toward their tent.

His frown deepened. "Sterling has seen more war and bloodshed than someone his age ought to. It breaks a man."

"You seem unaffected."

"We all have different ways of coping. For me… My heart has become numb to the bloodshed. It takes a bit of coaxing from my wife to unravel the scars."

Her worry for Sterling increased, and she only wished to climb back into bed with him and hold him until all his scars healed. "Will he recover?"

Gilberd remained silent for a beat too long, as if horrifying images flashed across his mind. It was clear he wanted to be alone. "One never forgets their experience during war. But with time, he will heal. He always does. It was for the best that you never had to witness the pain inflicted upon his soul after each battle. It might have broken you, too."

He said nothing more, and she took the cue to leave him be. She tied her hair up and ventured into the large nurses' tent where the wounded soldiers' groans of pain were the loudest. One man, in particular, released a blood-curdling scream at having the bone set in his leg. Kathleen grimaced at the amount of blood trickling down to his ankle. He'd never walk well again, if at all.

"Where can I assist?" she asked one of the nurses, whose eyes widened.

"You are the queen, Your Highness." The nurse dipped into a quick curtsy. "I would not have you labor beside us."

"Hogwash. I have done my fair share of nursing." She surveyed the rows of makeshift beds on the ground, locating an unconscious man with a bandage tight around a severed arm. The wound had already bled through and needed a change. "I will start by changing his wrappings. I expect you to have several more tasks for me when I am done."

Without waiting for her reply, she located a basket of clean bandages and carefully rewrapped the man's wound. He whimpered in his sleep, but otherwise remained unconscious.

For the next several hours and well into early morning, she tended to the wounded until she could no longer hold her eyelids open. She cleaned the blood from her hands before climbing back into bed beside Sterling, who was still in a deep sleep. She kissed the tip of his nose and succumbed to sleep herself.

Only four or five hours passed when she woke again in the light of early morning to find Sterling still asleep. He must have been completely exhausted to slumber so soundly for so long. It worried her. Had he sustained any injuries she hadn't seen in the dark last night? She'd witnessed soldiers getting dragged down by the darkness of their own minds, never to wake again.

A shudder raced through her, but she forced it away.

She bit her lip when she noticed a scar on his bare shoulder right where he'd been struck by an arrow on their wedding day, as well as several smaller scars sustained from other battles. She slowly peeled back the bedroll with the intention of slipping out without waking him but gasped as she spotted a large bruise on his side. Her hand flew to her mouth, her heart racing. Forcing her mind to remain clear-headed, she inspected the wound closer. The skin was a deep purple, meaning it had happened recently. She recalled all of his symptoms from yesterday—dizziness, weakness, fatigue. He hadn't expressed any signs of nausea, fainting, chest pain, or bleeding from his mouth or nose.

Hopefully, the wound was nothing serious, but rather only affected the bruised area. She would check on him periodically just in case.

Silently slipping out of the bedroll, she tied her hair up again and got back to work.

Chapter Thirteen

A groan escaped Sterling's mouth as he rolled over onto his back. His side ached fiercely as if a hundred small needles pierced him. The wound throbbed in tune with his heartbeat, and he only wished sleep would drag him back into the darkness.

At least until he remembered Kathleen and what had happened last night.

His eyes flew open, but to his dismay, she was nowhere to be seen. Her sweet floral scent lingered in the bedroll next to him, and he breathed it in, memorizing the smell of her.

Despite the raging pain in his side, he smiled at the thought of his beautiful wife. Since his parents' deaths, he had felt so alone. But Kathleen filled the empty hole inside his heart. She more than just filled it—her kindness and mere presence made his happiness overflow like a brook springing through cracks in a riverbed.

Desire to see her again his motivation, he grimaced through the pain as he dressed and smoothed his wild bed hair—which was mostly Kathleen's fault—but he paused when something caught his eye.

His eyebrows furrowed as he moved closer to what appeared to be a painting, half-hidden from view. Shock jolted his heart when he recognized the painting as himself, so realistic that he could have been looking into a mirror. Each strand of the hair was incredibly detailed, his coy smile peeking out from behind his white sleeve, his arms above his head. The blue of his eyes was intense, the obvious focus of the painting.

Did his eyes really look like that? It had been so long since he'd looked into a mirror.

Even more impressive, had Kathleen truly painted this? He had already known of her artistic skill, but this went far beyond his expectations.

The desire to see her hit him hard. He pushed aside the tent flap, grinding his teeth to endure the pain of each step. He stopped for a moment, craning his neck to search over the heads of soldiers and nurses. Immediately, his heart lit up like a ray of sunshine breaking through storm clouds when he spotted a head of honey-brown hair. Kathleen wore her hair in a bun, several shorter strands falling into her face as she carried a cauldron of water and hung it over the fire. His breath fled him as he watched her rest for a moment, facing the fire. How had he become so lucky to have a wife so beautiful, so talented, so incredible?

He approached her from behind, and she jumped as he wrapped his arms around her waist. But then she smiled when he pressed an endearing kiss to her cheek.

"Good morning, Kathleen," he said into her ear.

Excited chills raced up his spine when she placed her hands on top of his and craned her neck back to look at him. Her eyes captivated him, stealing the words right from his mouth.

"Are you intent on scaring the bones out of me this early in the day?"

"Mhmm." He continued to hold her, warmth seeping into him from her gentle touch. She leaned back against him, easily coaxing his smile out. It felt so nice to hold his wife close. Her mere presence filled him with immense comfort.

His heart skipped in his chest when she wrapped her arm around the back of his neck and pulled him down for a kiss. Her lips tasted sweeter than honey straight from the hive.

She broke the kiss all too soon, though her gaze remained fixed on him. "I love you, Sterling," she whispered.

"Pardon?" His stomach twisted in surprise, and his eyes widened. For a moment, he wondered if he'd heard her wrong. She loved him? But...but...but...

Heat rushed up his neck and into his ears. Genuine sincerity glowed in her expression. He'd only dreamed of hearing those words from her mouth for so long. But now his tongue refused to work, and he reckoned he looked like an idiot just staring at her as he did.

"I love when you do that," she said, continuing to speak quietly.

"Do what?"

"The thing with your eyebrows." She stood on her toes and kissed the space just above his nose. "It has been one of my favorite qualities about you since we first met."

"Oh?" A smile spread across his face, a welcome action after the horrors he'd experienced over the past week. It felt nice to smile again. "*One* of your favorite qualities? What are the others?"

She gently touched his chest, right over his heart. "You have always been very sweet and thoughtful."

"And handsome?" he teased.

Now it was her turn to blush. "I never said that."

"No? The painting in our tent says it all."

Her eyes widened. "Oh, drat. The painting... I forgot about it. That was supposed to be private."

"I rather like it. You are exceptionally skilled."

Her blush deepened, but in an instant, it vanished, replaced by a look of pure rage. Oh no… Had he missed another one of her hints? But as he thought back on their conversation just now, he didn't think she had given him any hints, subtle or otherwise.

"When were you going to tell me about your injury?" she fumed as she faced him more fully. "I saw it this morning. It looks bad. What happened?"

He released her waist, the color draining from his face as memories attacked his mind against his will. Screams. Cries of pain. Bloodshed. He glanced back and forth across the camp, glad that most soldiers were either still sleeping or they were occupied with eating breakfast.

Running a hand across the back of his neck, he shrugged. "I'm fine."

"Tell me," she demanded with a piercing glare. He couldn't help but give in with that look.

"I got hit by a mace. The impact threw me off my horse. But as you can see, I'm fine. You needn't be angry with me."

Distress grew in her eyes. "I wish you would have told me, Sterling."

"I didn't want to worry you."

She shook her head and grabbed his hand, gently cradling it against her face. "I've worried about you since the moment you were struck by an arrow on our wedding day. You don't have to endure it alone."

Once again, he stared at her like an idiot. For so long, he'd always been alone, and it wasn't until he had formed a friendship with Gilberd when things had started to change. But it wasn't the same having the captain of the guard as a friend, because in the end, Gilberd still served his king.

"Your Highnesses," a voice said, and when Kathleen dropped Sterling's hand, he felt the loss of contact like a severed limb.

He turned his head to find Gilberd with a bowed head, though a flash of excitement gleamed in his eyes.

Continuing, the captain said, "Armandy has approached from the west."

"Another attack?" His expression became more serious, and he waited on the tips of his toes to gather his weapons together.

"No. They bear a white flag of surrender."

Surprise jolted through his body, and he repeated Gilberd's words in his mind over and over in case he'd heard them wrong. "Surrender? Is it a trick?"

Gilberd shook his head. "They've suffered many casualties. I reckon they're ready to cease bloodshed. Would you have us ride out to meet their surrender?"

For a long moment, he didn't answer. To ride out would put him and his men at risk should their enemies use the surrender as a trick to draw them out. But if it truly wasn't a trick, and they meant to give up their war efforts…

He couldn't waste this opportunity, no matter the outcome. He needed his lands to be safe. For his people. For Kathleen.

He smiled.

For his future children.

At last, he returned Gilberd's hopeful gaze and nodded. "We'll ride out within the hour."

"Please be safe," Kathleen said, worry running rampant in her eyes.

He gently squeezed her fingers and gave her a reassuring smile. "Even Armandy wouldn't commit perfidy during war. Even so, I give you my word that I'll be careful."

Despite the flag of surrender, he still planned to outfit himself in armor, just in case negotiations didn't work out. He followed Gilberd to the armory tent while the other soldiers in the camp hurried to dress themselves in their own armor and weapons.

Gilberd raised an eyebrow high the moment Kathleen was out of earshot.

"What?" Sterling asked.

"You can't deny it now. Something happened with Kathleen."

He rolled his eyes and pushed him in the shoulder. "Shut it, Gilberd. My married life is none of your business."

His friend burst into laughter and shoved him right back. "I suppose that means the annulment is called off. You'll finally get an heir."

"Let's just focus on me not dying first, yes?"

Chapter Fourteen

Sterling took a deep breath as he stared across the vast green field separating his army from Armandy's. King Harold stared at him from where he perched on his horse, and Sterling stared right back. The white flag of surrender flapped in the breeze. Gray rain clouds hung over their heads as if holding their breath before a storm. No one dared to move a muscle.

"I don't feel comfortable with you going out there unarmed," Gilberd said beside him, startling him out of the too-quiet atmosphere. "It would take only one well-aimed arrow to kill you."

"I am all too aware of that fact." A shudder ran down his body. Whether it stemmed from fear or from the sudden chill, he wasn't sure. "If something happens, tell Kathleen—"

"—tell her yourself, sire."

He took a deep breath and let it out slowly as he surveyed the army standing behind King Harold. They still had many soldiers. Why the surrender?

The enemy king threw his leg over the side of his horse and landed on the ground before making a show of handing his weapons to a soldier beside him. Sterling swallowed nervously as he followed suit. He handed the captain his dagger and unstrapped his sword from his belt before handing that over as well. He'd need to approach the enemy unarmed.

Nothing could prepare him for what he was about to face.

As soon as King Harold began to approach, Sterling slid from his horse, trying to ignore the throbbing pain in his side. But the throbbing wound pulsed with each uncomfortable step he took toward the other man. His heart burst to life inside his chest like drums pounding amidst a war. He took off his helmet and tucked it beneath one arm, leaving him exposed to take an arrow to the head.

Leading his men into war was far less frightening than this.

At last, he stood only a few feet away from the Armandy king. The man's bushy red eyebrows pulled together, his copper mustache tinged with gray hairs moving as his mouth twitched.

"You are but a young man," King Harold murmured, stroking his jaw. "I expected someone…much older."

"That someone would have been my father should he still be alive." His nostrils flared against his will as his anger surfaced. He hated this man before him more than anything in the world. He had taken so much from him.

"How old are you, son?"

Son?

He only barely kept himself from spitting at the man's feet. How dare he look down on him when he was the one holding the white flag.

"Twenty."

The man stroked his beard yet again. "You were only eighteen when the war began. Only three years younger than Nicholas."

Attempting to shift the topic, Sterling said, "You have come to us bearing a white flag. What brought this truce to fruition?"

At the mention, a deep, torturous sadness entered the king's eyes. "I lost someone dear to me."

"You killed *my* family," he reminded in a not-so-gentle tone.

"And now you have killed mine. My son, Nicholas, was run through by your sword. Do you recall the last fight with him? He had been carrying a mace."

His face blanched, his fingers reflexively touching the tender spot on his side beneath his armor. But as he remembered this was war, his expression hardened. "If you had only called for a truce much earlier, we wouldn't have had to lose many good men."

"Indeed." King Harold stared at the ground with a faraway look. The wrinkles around his eyes deepened with each passing moment. A tense silence followed as both armies watched the other warily. Finally, the king spoke, "My feud with your father has been a long one, starting over a woman. I used to court your mother. We had plans to wed."

His eyebrows furrowed in surprise. He'd never heard this story. Curiosity took a hold of him against his better judgement. "What happened?"

The other king's mouth turned downward in a frown. "She fell in love with another man."

"My father."

"Yes."

Sterling clenched his fists as he remembered the pale, lifeless face of his mother, taken too early in death. "Your assassins killed my mother."

"She was never meant to die. We had only meant to kill your father."

"And what of your feud with *me*?" He was suddenly glad he didn't have a weapon on him, because at the moment, he felt close to losing his temper. "How have I wronged you?"

Other than killing Nicholas. But they both knew he spoke of before the war.

King Harold's eyes flashed dangerously, but a moment later, it disappeared. He answered with only a name, but it sent shivers racing down his spine. "Kathleen de Clare."

"You leave my wife out of this," he growled.

"I am not here to fight," the king said, holding up his hands in a display of peace. "I am here to call a truce. Our reasons for war have died with my son. He petitioned Kathleen's father for her hand, but her father said she'd already been spoken for. We were too late to stop the wedding."

He closed his eyes as he bit back words of hatred, but then they flashed open again when he remembered he was still a target. He didn't dare lower his guard. This man deserved to die. He deserved for his army to get trampled and slaughtered.

But how many of his own men would get killed in such a retaliation? Over a woman? Or rather, two women? And the pursuit of land. The war may have started many years ago between his father and the king of Armandy, but the resentment and hatred in the man's heart had kept the war aflame long after the death of his parents. He suspected Kathleen was only a small portion of their underlying reasons to prolong the fighting.

A truce was the only option, as much as he hated the idea of allowing this brute to live.

"What have you brought to offer with the truce?" Sterling asked, keeping his fists at his sides.

Slowly, King Harold reached into a compartment inside his armor. Subsequently, a chorus of singing metal erupted behind Sterling as his entire army drew a weapon. Harold's men kept their weapons sheathed.

When the other king pulled out a scroll, Sterling lifted a hand to placate his men, and another chorus of screeching metal commenced as they sheathed their weapons.

He took the scroll and unrolled it, scanning the words scrawled across the parchment. Armandy would gift a portion of their lands to Edilann. They would cease fighting and pull their armies out of Sterling's lands. They would also give a sum of money to help Edilann rebuild what had been lost to the war.

"I notice you are not demanding anything from me," Sterling said when he lifted his gaze.

"Such is the way of the one waving the white flag. We are losing much from calling a truce. But I desire to fight no longer."

Again, the haggardness loomed heavily in the wrinkles on the man's face, in the slump in his shoulders, in the emptiness in his eyes. For a moment, guilt slammed its fist into Sterling's gut. He'd done this. He'd killed Nicholas.

But…killing Nicholas had ended the war. There would be no more bloodshed. Kathleen would be safe. He felt immense guilt, yes. But not regret.

"I will sign your treaty," he said. "Have you a quill?"

King Harold motioned with his hand, and a boy promptly scurried in their direction, the pack on his back bouncing with each step as if he were a horse on a trail run. Out of breath, the boy reached into the pack and pulled out a bottle of ink and a quill bent out of shape. He handed the quill with a sheepish smile to the king, who dipped it into the ink and signed his name at the bottom of the treaty.

When the other man handed him the quill, Sterling took a deep, steadying breath. He could hardly believe it. After two years of moving from battlefield to battlefield, it would finally end with a single brushstroke.

King Sterling Winfield

There, he'd done it.

He lifted the treaty into the air for each army to see. Shouts of triumph shook the ground, and Sterling couldn't help but smile at his own elation. No more fighting. No more bloodshed.

They'd won the war.

Shouts of triumph, gleeful laughter, and expressions of relief filled the camp upon Sterling's return, and Kathleen couldn't help but join in on their joy. She laughed as she twirled around with Gilberd while the captain simply grinned, and then she clung on tight to Sterling around the neck.

His hands held her waist. But he didn't return her joy. Instead, he wore a pinched expression full of guilt and regret. Her smile fell.

"Sterling, what's the matter?"

For several long moments, he simply stared at her, his jaw working as if trying to figure out what to say. Finally, he took her hand and pulled her away from everyone else while they celebrated with dance, song, and drink. Worry knotted her stomach. Sterling should be overjoyed. Why didn't he seem happy?

They stopped beneath the shade of a tall, leafy tree, the foliage the color of deep emeralds. His fingers drummed on the pommel of his sword. And then he took a deep breath, letting it out slowly as he lifted his gaze.

"Kathleen, I'm terrified I will lose you over this." A tortured expression creased his brows. "I had no idea you had planned to wed Prince Nicholas."

The blood drained from her face. "How did you find out?"

"King Harold told me. When you first arrived on our docks two years ago, I thought you were disappointed because I was short and boyish and uncertain. But perhaps it was only a part of the reason." His throat bobbed up and down. "Should I have left you alone? Did you love him?"

Her lips parted, her eyes slowly growing into large orbs as she managed to link what he wasn't saying. Armandy had attacked on their *wedding* day.

No, no, no!

She held her hands to her mouth and whispered. "Am I the reason for this war? Is this my fault?"

"No," he firmly replied. He reached out to her but dropped his hand just as quickly. "You are not responsible for someone else's actions. And this war, this feud, has been going on for far longer than I've been alive."

The knots in her stomach loosened as she leaned against the trunk of the tree. She wouldn't have been able to live with herself if she had been the reason why so many good men had been injured or lost their lives.

Yet, Sterling still didn't touch her, and the anxiety still lingered in his expression.

"You didn't answer my question," he murmured. "Did you love Prince Nicholas? Did I steal you from a marriage that would have made you happy?"

Oh, Sterling.

Sadness and regret filled his eyes as he waited for her answer. He wanted the truth. And she would give him the truth. All of it. "I liked him quite a bit. I could have loved him given the chance. Things hadn't gone that far."

"And what about now? What are your feelings?"

"For him?"

He nodded. Clearly, he still thought he could lose her over this new information. She had to make him see reason.

"I love *you*, Sterling," she whispered with conviction. "Not him. I haven't spoken to him since before our wedding. The thought of him sickens me after what Armandy did to your parents. Did to you."

Yet, her words didn't seem to mollify him. A haunted expression still shone in his eyes, in the pinch of his mouth, in the working of his jaw.

"What happened?" She reached out to touch his hand. "What aren't you telling me?"

He stared down at their touching hands for far too long. But when he finally spoke, he didn't look her in the eye. "I didn't know it was him." His voice became husky. Filled with emotion. "I killed him, Kathleen. It ended the war. But I killed him. Forgive me. I never meant to cause you distress."

Her lips parted in surprise, the breath halting in her lungs. Her hand dropped from his, hanging limp at her side. *Sterling killed Nicholas?*

She blinked several times, trying to wrap her mind around his words. Of course, she knew bloodshed was a part of war. Inevitable stains on everyone's souls. But for him to outright admit to it about the man she'd been fond of? The man she'd shared a kiss with and the man she'd once hoped to marry?

"Forgive me," he murmured. "I'm so sorry, Kathleen. So very sorry."

But then the shock wore off as her gaze darted to his side and what lay hidden behind layers of armor. He'd been so secretive about his injury, but she couldn't help but wonder…

She lifted her hand to his face, her fingers gentle against his cheek. Haunted shadows rested beneath his eyes. Within his soul. "Did Nicholas give you that wound?"

He swallowed and nodded. "I didn't know it had been him until today. If I had just looked harder. If I had only noticed the royal emblem on his breastplate. But all I saw was him swinging his mace, about to take Gilberd's head off. I just acted—"

He inhaled sharply when she embraced him and held on tight. She only wished his steady beating heart pressed against her ear rather than the cold metal of his armor. "I asked Gilberd about the injury while you were sleeping. He told me the blow nearly killed you. That they almost didn't get your dented armor off in time." At the terrifying thought, she held on even tighter. "You saved his life. I almost lost my friend. I almost lost the man I love, too."

"But I—"

"You saved his life." She pulled away, only to grip his armored elbows. "That was an honorable thing. I am only relieved you are alive." She kissed his wrist, his palm, his fingers. "There is nothing to forgive."

Sterling's lips parted as if in surprise. "You told me that you couldn't forgive me yet. For all I put you through."

Happy for his warm, sturdy hands in her grip, she held his palm against her cheek. "And I'm telling you now that there is no longer anything to forgive."

"Kathleen…" The haunted expression melted from his eyes as he pulled her close and crushed her against him. A loving embrace. A healing embrace. They had weathered this storm together. And they would continue to weather any storms that may come their way.

"I love you," he murmured into her hair. "I am so lucky to have you."

She held on tight to him, grateful he had survived the war and they could be together again. "I am yours, Sterling. Only yours."

Chapter Fifteen

When the war had first started, Kathleen had assumed she would be one among hundreds of people waving handkerchiefs in the air, welcoming her soldiers, and husband, back after a victorious battle.

But instead, she rode sidesaddle alongside Sterling, him wearing his armor and her a dress, both with their crowns atop their heads. Had she stayed at the palace as she'd originally wanted, she would have twiddled her thumbs and wasted away each day in worry. Instead, she'd made a difference, too. Although difficult to endure the abbey, she was grateful that she'd been able to contribute in some way.

Whistles, shouts of triumph, and song lifted into the air as they rode past, flanked on either side by soldiers and guards. Handkerchiefs of all shapes, colors, and sizes waved in the air. Relief. Happiness. Victory.

A soldier in front of them abandoned his horse as he hopped down and flew into the arms of a teary eyed woman. Another soldier accepted a handkerchief from a smiling, hopeful young woman.

The smiles and laughter of children brought tears to her eyes when they tackled their returning father with a fierce embrace.

With Gilberd as their escort, she and Sterling rode beneath the castle gates where villagers and members of the court leaned over stone ledges to throw flower petals over their heads. Kathleen laughed joyously from within the shower of silky petals. Sterling reached for her hand and lifted it in the air. Deafening cheers followed.

She smiled at him. He smiled back with the half-grin she loved so much.

"Mirabelle!" Gilberd shouted moments before he slid off his horse and threw his arms around a petite brown-haired woman with a toddler on her hip. The children clinging to her skirts hugged their father around the legs and waist. The oldest of their children looked to be nine years old.

Kathleen inhaled sharply when she spotted a tuft of brown and white fur peeking out from behind Mirabelle. A sob of relief and happiness lodged in her throat. She released Sterling's hand and slid off the horse, stumbling several steps as she ran toward her dog.

"Bear!"

The dog's ears perked up at the sound of his name moments before his tail started wagging ceaselessly. He barked excitedly, jumped up on her and almost knocked her over, and covered her face in slobbery kisses.

"You remember me!" She kissed the top of his head, marveling at how big he had grown in her absence. On all fours, his head likely reached her waist now.

"Sorry," Mirabelle apologized before she ordered the mutt to sit. "I tried to train him not to jump up on people, but he's just too excited to see you."

Sterling approached and scratched the dog behind the ears. Bear's tongue fell lopsidedly out of his mouth as he panted and wagged his tail. "So, this is the infamous Bear I've heard so much about. I have a long road ahead of me if I want to gain Kathleen's affection over yours."

She laughed and hugged Sterling's arm, her lips falling into a coy smile. She met his blue-eyed gaze and murmured, "You may be closer than you think."

He swallowed, his eyes shimmering with what appeared to be gratitude mixed with relief and happiness.

"Welcome home, Kathleen."

Her eyes smarted as she slipped her fingers into his. "It's good to finally be back."

Sterling gazed down at his wife, all too aware of the complete adoration in his eyes as he danced with her around the spacious ballroom. He didn't care that everyone was watching. He only cared about the lovely woman in his arms.

When Kathleen looked over her shoulder for the dozenth time, he chuckled. "Stop doing that."

"Doing what?"

"Your eyes are anxiously darting about. What are you afraid of?"

Finally, she turned her attention back to him, nervousness sparking in those pretty blue eyes of hers. "I apologize. The last time we danced, you were struck by an arrow. I am having unpleasant flashbacks of that night."

He squeezed her hand and pulled her close enough to whisper in her ear. "I have the palace grounds heavily patrolled. No one will get in or out without my men knowing of it first. I promise you are safe."

"And you?"

A warmth surged through him at her concern for him. For so long, he'd been alone. First, his parents had been killed. And then he'd been separated from his wife. But no longer. He loved this woman dearly. "And me."

The rigidness in her shoulders relaxed, her taut lips pulling into a smile as he spun her around and pulled her back to him while avoiding the other dancers on the floor. Now that his body was no longer juvenile and awkward, he found dancing had become a little easier. If only barely. Kathleen still outshined him by far.

"It has been ten weeks since we were reunited," Kathleen said, her smile growing even wider, though a spark of mischief lighted in her eyes. "A lot has happened since then."

"It has." Rebuilding from the damage and costs of war had been no easy feat, and it would take longer still for their kingdom to flourish in peace, but it was now a possibility. "I'm not sure what to do with myself when I'm no longer hopping from one battle to the next."

"I have an idea of what you can do."

The light in her eyes flared once more with mischief, and he wondered for a moment if he'd missed one of her hints. Had he?

"And what would that be?" he asked cautiously.

"I would like you to put together a room facing the sunrise with a beautiful view of the gardens."

His eyebrows scrunched together as he pulled back to look at her. "You already have an art room. Does it not suffice?"

She laughed at him, and he was now absolutely certain he'd missed a hint. But at least she wasn't angry. Yet. "No, no. The room isn't for me. We will have a visitor in seven months. We must get the room ready."

Now he stared back at her with confusion leaking from every one of his pores. He studied the amused upturn of her lips and the playful sparks in her eyes. "In seven months? But it will be winter. Who would visit us when the roads aren't passable?"

"Oh my, Sterling," she said in an exasperated tone with a roll of her eyes, though the smile didn't disappear from her face. "What is seven months plus two?"

"Nine…"

He gasped suddenly and misstepped, but she quickly covered his blunder with a graceful swish of her skirts. "What?" he choked. He stopped dancing, his eyes wide as his gaze darted toward her belly. There was no bump yet, but her joyous laughter confirmed what he suspected. "You are with child?"

He said it a little too loudly, as more than one person gasped before a buzz of excited chatter swarmed throughout the room.

"Yes," she laughed, kissing his palm. "And it seems everyone in the kingdom will know it before the sun goes down tonight."

Excitement shot up from the floor and struck his heart. Shock. Joy. Elation. Bewilderment. Twenty years didn't seem at all old enough to have a child yet, but in the past two years, he felt like he had aged a decade. He swore to himself he would be a good and loving father.

And if Kathleen agreed, then that child wouldn't have to grow up alone as he had either.

"A father…" He ran a hand down his face as emotion overcame him. "I am going to be a father."

"And I, a mother. I am so happy, Sterling."

A delighted sheen misted her eyes, and he couldn't help himself as he kissed each of her eyelids and then her sweet mouth. He held her face between his palms as he gazed at her in earnest. "I love you, Kathleen." He pecked her lips again. "And I'll show you just how much."

He pulled her by the hand to the patio leading outside, and into the garden beneath the sunset sky. A brilliant array of oranges, yellows, and pinks burst to life above. A sweet aroma picked up around them as they entered the rose garden, with every color of flower imaginable guiding him forward. He stopped before the bushes of pink roses and cut one free using the knife on his belt. This fresh one could soon join the dried, crisp rose he'd given her on their wedding day, saved and now nestled on a shelf in their room where they could both see it every day.

A beautiful smile lit up her face when he presented the gift to her, the sheen in her eyes returning once more. She twirled the flower between her fingers while inhaling its sweet scent.

"You know the way to my heart."

ABOUT THE AUTHOR

Sydney Winward is a fantasy and paranormal romance author who dabbles in the occasional historical fiction. She loves building complex worlds filled with magic, strong characters, and emotional stories that can make you laugh and cry.

Sydney is the author of the Sunlight and Shadows Series and the best-selling Bloodborn Series, and when she's not writing, she's reading, thinking about stories, or going on adventures with her children. She lives in Utah with her husband and three amazing kids.

www.sydneywinward.com